Ah, romance!

We all love falling in love. We all enjoy watching those two friends who *everyone* knows belong together finally get it over with and start dating.

Partners in Romance features tales of new friends-with-potential, people thrown together by circumstance, neighbors with spark, and much, much more.

Just like in real life, dogs fan romantic sparks into a flame. Mature lovebirds want happiness for the younger generation. Humor plays a vital role, especially when it comes to love's secret recipe.

With people starting out in life or making long-desired changes, hearts recognize each other.

Of course, all romance features dream chasing, and a good Happily Ever After.

Come along for the adventure as eight couples discover each other, and the promise of the beginning!

The Changes Cascade

Near Future Forward (with Jason A. Adams)

Dispatches from the Galaxy: A Space Opera Novella Trio

Dangerous Days on a Pleasure Planet

Storms of Future Past:

Dreaming the Storm

Joining the Storm

Into the Storm

Fighting the Storm

Storms of the Heart

Storms of Future Past Omnibus

Voices Through Time:

Songs in the Mountain

Secrets in the Land

Sorrows in the Earth

Walking the Ghosts

The Odd Society:

Independent by Means of Magic

Protected by Means of Magic

Collections:

Fantastic Shorts: Volume 1

Fantastic Shorts: Volume 2

Fantastic Shorts: Volume 3

Escape into Romance

Stepping Out of Reality

Facing Down Extraordinary

Hacking Cybercrime

Investigations Beyond Belief

Passages in the Real World

Fantastic Side Trips

A Kaleidoscope of Cat Tales

A Tapestry of Holiday Tales

Aunties Among Us

Four-Legged Heroes

Anthologies *with Jason A. Adams*:

Shadows Mountain Deep

Uncommon Holidays

Partnership in Crime

More great reads from Jason A. Adams

www.JasonAdamsBooks.com

Novellas:

Agonist

Collections and Anthologies:

Normally Fantastic

On the Case!

Capeless Heroes

Through the Squirrel Tree

Tales From the Squirrel Garden: Volume 1

(with Kari Kilgore)

Partnership in Crime

Shadows Mountain Deep

Near Future Forward

Uncommon Holidays

JASON A. ADAMS
KARI KILGORE

Partners in ROMANCE

Spiral Publishing, Ltd.

For Karen Adams and Clinas Kilgore

Both voracious readers of romance

CONTENTS

SWEET SPARKS OF THE BEGINNING

KARI KILGORE AND JASON A. ADAMS

Kari:

Writing short romance stories, like romance itself, is often a tricky dance.

As in all romance, we meet the two potential partners and get a good strong hint of how they react to each other. Those sparks and tingles and awareness that *something* is happening are vital parts of why we read romance in the first place.

Stories that tend toward the longer side can get into all the satisfying conflicts we love to read about rather than experience for ourselves. Tension when characters try to resist what readers and often their friends already know—they're meant for each other.

And of course, joy when they finally recognize how great they are together.

Short stories often don't get into those conflicts as much by definition. Only one of the stories in *Partners in Romance* breaks six thousand words, and barely at that.

So here you'll find stories with a variety of characters who focus on the possibility. The delicious sensation that this time *feels* different. Each person smooths the rough edges for the other, calms the worries and fears.

And both believe whatever comes up in the years ahead, they'll work through it all together.

One or two of the tales from both me and Jason (my partner in romance since 1990) might just bring touches of our own romantic reality into fiction.

I truly hope you enjoy reading these short, sweet treats as much as we do.

Jason:

And they lived happily ever after.

When I was a young lad, these words ended many of my favorite stories. Now that I'm a much older lad, my favorite stories still end with the sentiment, if not the same exact words.

Romance is one of the basic human desires. Kari and I both enjoy reading and writing these sweet tales—stories that remind us that love happens. Often when you least expect it.

Sometimes surprising, often overwhelming, the

spark of new attraction and new love is always a thrill.

Especially when that new attraction and new love promises a long and loving relationship that just might last a lifetime.

Partners in
ROMANCE

The Sweetest TROUBLE

KARI KILGORE

AUTHOR OF WALKING THE GHOSTS AND INTENTIONS

For Jason

*Who shares my love of adventure
and of staying home*

CHAPTER 1

*J*osh Waldron wandered barefoot around his new temporary apartment, counting his steps, listening to the echoes in the nearly empty space. Wondering how long it would take to feel like home.

The relocation agency had done an amazing job finding this place—a beautifully converted factory loft not far from downtown Atlanta.

Mellow hardwood floors throughout, salvaged from an old school gym. Concrete countertops in the kitchen and baths, all inset with old skeleton keys and bits of stained glass and gears and springs rescued from the factory.

The non-stinky paint they'd used lived up to its name. The only thing he smelled was the lemongrass of his own deodorant.

Close to the MARTA transit line that would take

Josh on a quick ride to his new job in a couple of days. Plenty of parking under the building for those unlucky enough to have to dive into the whirlpool of traffic every morning and evening.

The builders had managed to retain the retro-cool vibe of the hundred-year-old brick building while bringing in touches of pure modern. Josh had already taken himself from the third floor upstairs to the roof to see the huge array of solar panels and solar water-heating tanks, perfect for an already hot and sunny mid-May in Georgia.

From what he'd heard and read, the massive black water tanks and gleaming rectangles of blue and silver would be every bit as effective in February down here.

From the roof, he could see what looked like a gigantic forest all around him, broken here and there by the nearby train lines and the three huge interstate highways that bordered and defined Metro Atlanta. As for the city itself, the clustered glassy towers of downtown were closer, but he could see the sprawling jumble of big Midtown buildings in the distance as well.

He hadn't quite worked out what happened to uptown, why locals never seemed to capitalize downtown, or what Midtown was supposed to be halfway to. It was almost as mysterious as the dizzying number of streets with Peachtree in the name.

The factory loft developers had even managed to include a tree-lined courtyard with fire pits and two pools (one long enough for laps, the other twisty and clearly meant for relaxing), a community garden, and a half-mile-long running track around the complex. The track, the walking surface around the pool, and the raised gardening beds made with almost entirely recycled materials, of course.

Josh wondered how many pairs of shredded old sneakers had helped create the track's springy blue surface, so much more forgiving on his forty-something-year-old hips than concrete.

He brushed his fingertips over the mess of photos, paintings, and various other bit of art stacked up against the wall in the living room as he passed by. His preferred black metal frames were already warm from early Friday morning sunlight streaming in through the floor-to-ceiling windows.

Getting at least a few of those hung on the flat white walls would help give the place a homey touch, even if he did decide to send the rest right back to storage. Hanging anything on the solid wall of original tan brick might be more tricky, but the maintenance folks had sworn it could be done.

Josh walked back into the kitchen and opened the door of the stainless steel refrigerator again, staring at the mostly empty bright white shelves and spotless glass compartments.

Nope, the fridge hadn't managed to sprout whatever magical variety of food would satisfy his restless cravings in the ten minutes since he'd last checked. Only boring staples like milk, eggs, stuff for sandwiches. Fuel, basically, rather than anything more inspiring.

The only non-standard splurge for him was the decidedly non-organic non-dairy creamer he'd splashed into his coffee when he got up.

He purposely mussed his in-need-of-a-trim brown hair, wanting to make something at least *feel* lived-in. Comfortable. Familiar.

The echoing sound of his own footsteps only made the loneliness worse.

The move had been the right decision. Josh's mind—freed from the demands of a slowly dying relationship for the first time in eight years—understood that, and had reacted accordingly by leaping into action the second a concrete job offer in digital special effects materialized.

Josh and his mind had finally punched their ticket for the Life Change Express straight out of Nowhereville, Ohio, barely three weeks ago. After nearly three years of study, and a year after the end of his relationship with Mike. Josh had heard and heeded the advice to avoid big decisions right after a breakup. Even if that breakup had only been delayed by inertia.

Now here he was, within reach of his big city dreams.

Staring out the window at the city he'd chosen to dream in.

Hoping the whole thing would be worth facing alone.

Maybe if he repeated the mantra to his heart a few thousand more times (*the move was the right decision*), the message would finally sink in.

Movement down in the community garden caught his attention, and he gratefully accepted the distraction.

Several people milled around at the arched metal gateway to the garden, right before the broad graveled path split to pass through the neat and even rows of knee-high boxes. Josh didn't recognize anyone, but then he'd barely *met* anyone since moving in a few days ago. He could make out two men and three women, but not much else.

They did look like they were around his general age, at least from three stories up. Exactly the sorts of people he wanted to meet if he went by clothing and general attitude. Blue jeans, colorful t-shirts. A couple of floppy sunhats.

The willingness to work together to make the sprawling garden better for everybody, even if they were supposedly there for the short term, like Josh.

Nice as these apartments were, about a quarter of them were tiny, designed for people who would be moving out or moving on before too much time passed. Less than a thousand square feet, much less in some cases.

Josh had a small living room, bathroom, one bedroom, and the strangely large kitchen. Maybe that's where people were supposed to gather, if transient residents gathered at all.

He hadn't planned on needing any kind of temporary housing. Not years back when he'd starting daydreaming, then thinking, then planning this move into the next phase of his life.

He'd expected to be buying a house with Mike.

Not huddled in a glorified hotel and pretending he was fine with that. Acting like this half-new life, this rootless existence would suit him for more than a few weeks.

Pushed out of his hyper-focused plans and dreams and expectations by Mike's need for constant calm. Stability. Predictability.

And because it had taken Josh so long to recognize how his own growing need for change—and the fear that went along with it—left the two of them less compatible rather than more as the years passed.

Well, his longed-for change was finally here, and he wasn't about to huddle inside and try to avoid it now.

Josh shook himself, stepped into a pair of the shoes he'd lined up neatly beside the front door, and escaped the empty apartment.

CHAPTER 2

*K*eith Anders stared at the shovel in his hand, wondering how the hell he'd come all the way from a year spent back home on his family's Illinois farm to walking into a community garden on his first day in Atlanta. At least he wouldn't be dealing with a huge herd of sheep or mucking out a horse barn here.

At least he didn't think so.

The neat and orderly garden in front of him looked more like a botanical garden than one actual food came from. Precise graveled walkways almost wide enough to be driveways. Immaculate boxes made of some kind of recycled plastic boards that actually did look like wood. Geometric arrangements of pale heads of cabbage, darker leafy kale, and broccoli like miniature trees were backed by vines loaded with green beans, cucumbers, and melons cradled in little slings.

Keith figured the heat that hadn't quite arrived would take out lettuce and spinach and such before long. But he surprised himself by looking forward to what he might be able to coax out of the rich, nearly black soil well into the fall with an extra month before the killing frost.

The fluffy clouds in the deep blue sky overhead were punctuated by an amazing number of airplanes. He'd never seen so much traffic in the sky outside of New York City's airspace, and here almost all of it was heading to one vast airport.

But even with that and the never-ending traffic he knew ran through and around Atlanta, all he could smell as he walked deeper into the garden was that rich soil. The tart, pungent, *green* aroma of the thriving tomato vines he couldn't resist touching as he passed.

The jets high above left a faint roar, but what Keith mostly heard at ground level was his boots crunching in the gravels, the wind brushing his curly blond hair back and away from his face. The low hum of honeybees from the garden's colony working feverishly in the rows of red and purple flowers beyond the raised beds.

If Keith's latest escape from his farm-boy roots meant he had to come a long way south and end up right back in a garden patch, at least it was a beautiful one.

He'd just reached four played-out beds that had recently been full of radishes and early peas (complete with a rake and a huge half-barrel of compost for him to shovel in) when a man spoke from right behind him.

"Is this gardening thing voluntary? Or all the new residents assigned a turn, like chores?"

Keith turned and blinked, then smiled. This wasn't any of the other members of the informal garden committee he'd just met about an hour ago. For one thing, nice as they were, none of them looked anywhere *near* this good.

Mystery Guy stood a little shorter than Keith, just under six feet tall, with thick brown hair standing up in the most adorable bed-head mess. The tan khakis and light green dress shirt weren't as well suited for gardening as Keith's old jeans and ancient t-shirt, but the clothes certainly…fit well.

Mystery Guy looked strong, but not gym machine strong. Actual activity and getting out and doing things strong. Keith's favorite.

"Well, I just got here last night," Keith said. "So I'm not sure if garden duty is only for me or for everyone new. They haven't told me all the rules yet. I think they do that on purpose to keep the new folks off-balance."

Mystery Guy grinned. "We'll have to stick

together, then." He held out a big, square hand. "Josh Waldron. Got here a couple of days ago, but I must have snuck in under the chore radar."

Keith laughed and let Josh's hand swallow his in a warm, firm grip.

"Keith Anders. I made the mistake of admitting I grew up in farm country in southern Illinois. Or it could be because I volunteered so I could get out and meet people. I have to force myself to do that when I get to a new place sometimes."

Josh nodded and rolled his big green eyes. "Yeah, I have to force myself most of the time. It's usually worth it. I come from middle of nowhere Ohio, but I have exactly zero farm or garden experience myself. What exactly are you out here doing? Taking the dirt out of the boxes?"

Keith squatted beside the raised bed, pleased that Josh did the same.

"This isn't merely dirt," he said, gathering up a handful of the cool, slightly moist contents of the box. "Dirt gets in the corners and on the car and all over your nice clothes if you're not careful. What you're looking at here is soil. Nice quality, too. I'm adding compost to these four to feed it and make it even better for the next crops."

Josh grabbed a handful himself, squeezing it between his fingers. Keith smiled when Josh held it close to his nose and sniffed.

"Smells good. Not like chemicals, or what I've always heard you farmer types use for fertilizer."

"There *are* times of the year when a big farm doesn't smell quite so good." Keith wrinkled his nose. "You can just about taste the air. You generally don't get that in a nice garden space like this."

Josh sprinkled the soil back into the bed, brushed his hands together, and stood. He looked up at Keith under his eyebrows and smiled. A swarm of humming bees seemed to take flight in Keith's belly.

Gods, but this one was handsome.

"Since you're not actually shoveling shit," Josh said, "want some help? Or at least company and someone to talk to? I promise not to make too big a mess."

Keith handed the shovel over with a smile.

"You bet. I'll rake, and you shovel since you're not exactly dressed for messy work." Keith took a chance and put on his best imitation of a rich, Southern drawl. "So why don't you tell me, Josh, what brings an Ohio boy like you way down south to Georgia?"

CHAPTER 3

By the time all the compost was shoveled and raked into the garden beds, Josh was covered with sweat, wearing more of the soil than he wanted to admit, and had a nice set of blisters going on both hands.

He was also deep into a solid crush on Keith.

Not only was he good looking in a lanky, outdoorsy kind of way, with loopy blond curls and sparkling blue eyes only making it worse. He also had the dry, sarcastic sense of humor Josh hadn't even realized he was going to miss.

He knew very well that the Midwest wasn't a monolithic culture any more than the South was. Ohio and Illinois were hardly identical in their culture, politics, or even their landscapes.

But the voice and smartass attitude from somewhere close to home helped Josh feel a whole lot less homesick.

He settled the shovel into what looked like a wooden whiskey barrel cut in half, hoping he wouldn't have to carry it somewhere in front of Keith. His sore hands and achy shoulders wouldn't make much of a manly impression on anyone, much less a guy used to doing this kind of work all the time.

"Are you in one of the tiny apartments?" Josh said. "Mine is great, but barely room to turn around except in the cavern of a kitchen."

Keith tucked the rake in beside the shovel and brushed that gorgeous blond hair back.

"Not this time around, though I've lived in shoeboxes more than once. I'll be working from home a lot, but the main office is over in Decatur. Easy train ride or drive, so I guess I'll have at least a home base here for a while. One reason I went into software engineering is so I can pick up and move once I get enough experience."

Josh smiled, hoping his disappointment didn't show. Of course a guy this interesting would be moving on soon.

"Where would you go?" Josh said. "Atlanta's not exciting enough for you?" He groaned inside when he realized he sounded way too much like Mike.

Keith smiled and threw his arms out. "Where

wouldn't I go? I've been lucky enough to get to most of the states in the US and a bunch of other countries in my thirty-eight years, but I haven't even gotten started yet."

The words slipped out before Josh could stop them.

"Aren't you afraid sometimes?"

"Lots of times, sure," Keith said. "I was scared walking out here earlier, meeting a bunch of new people. I will be going in to work for the first time, too. But that's part of the thrill, isn't it? Taking that chance on something new."

Josh took a deep breath. That sounded a lot like his own words, trying to convince Mike to change with him.

Or maybe Josh had actually been trying to convince himself.

"That makes sense to me," Josh said. "Sometimes it just seems…easier to say than to do."

Keith shrugged. "I guess I just got into the habit after enough years of wishing I had a different life. I finally decided to *live* a different life. Listen, they're having kind of a meet and greet out in the courtyard later, around the pools. To welcome all us new kids. I've got to go shower off before I'll be fit for any kind of company. Want to meet me there, say at six?"

Josh looked down and brushed at the soil—now merely dirt, he supposed, since it was where it shouldn't be—decorating his fairly nice clothes. Being asked out even on a semi-date for the first time in nearly ten years threw him for a loop.

And it felt damn good, too.

"Sure, that sounds great," he said, meeting Keith's gaze. "I'll be there. Maybe you can tell me more about your travels. I guess I'm getting a late start since I'm already forty-three, but I *am* finally out of Ohio."

Keith touched Josh's shoulder, and a jolt of heat went straight from there to a couple of extremely attentive parts of Josh's anatomy.

"It's never too late, Josh. Never. See you at six."

Josh watched Keith walk away, enjoying the view too much to move until a very friendly woman on a four-wheeler came to collect the huge compost bucket and the tools. About the time he made it out of the community garden, his phone buzzed in his pocket.

The timing, as usual, was the best and the worst it possibly could be.

Hey Ry.

Hope all is going well down in Atlanta and it's everything you hoped for.

Stay safe. M

Josh sighed. Sometimes he wished he and Mike were on typical ex silent treatment behavior. Staying friends made all kinds of sense when they lived in the same small town and almost all their friends were shared. And when Josh had been too hard-core focused on his studies and the job hunt to even think about dating.

Now though, the first contact in a few weeks coming through right after he'd made arrangements for what he sincerely hoped *was* an actual date simply magnified how awkward and strange these random messages could be.

He climbed the black metal staircase set against the tan brick inside wall up to his tiny apartment, talking under his breath the whole time.

"You will not let this upset you. It's normal to be afraid and still *do the thing*. And you will sure as *shit* not get so afraid that you decide to skip this get-together where you'll have more time to talk to your very handsome new neighbor!"

Because he could hate it as much as he wanted to, but Josh *was* afraid. Scared he'd jumped into big city/new job way too fast. Scared he'd left the only long-term relationship he was ever going to have. Never mind that neither of them had been happy for a while.

Scared he was going to get involved with someone brave and adventurous (and gorgeous), only to have Keith break it off because Josh was too timid after all.

And maybe worst of all, what if he and Keith really did hit it off? Fell really hard, maybe even decided to get married? But the next time Keith needed to leave, Josh was too terrified to go with him.

Then, according to this dark fantasy about a thousand miles down the road from reality, Keith might just leave.

Kind of like Josh had left Mike.

What if Josh wasn't much braver than Mike after all? What if he'd already used up his precious store of courage leaving Ohio, and Atlanta was as far as he could manage to get? No matter the cost?

Josh closed his apartment door, pushed his sore back muscles against the cool metal, and thumped the back of his head against it a couple of times for good measure. He got his phone back out.

Time to nip this nasty anxiety cesspool in the bud before it could really settle in and drag him down with it.

Hey Mike.

All good here, going really well. Excited to finally be getting started.

Hope all is well with you.

Take care. R

Josh set the phone to do-not-disturb-except-for-emergencies, stepped out of his shoes, and went to get ready for his semi-date.

CHAPTER 4

$\mathcal{K}$eith walked around the tan brick-lined courtyard, cold gin and tonic mostly untouched in his hand, doing his best not to keep an eye out for Josh a good twenty minutes before they'd agreed to meet.

There were plenty of other distractions available to him, even in a small crowd of about fifty people. Discussions of the history of the old factory, including how you could tell where the bricks underfoot had come from by the way they were grouped together into a two-dimensional map. Chatter about the nightlife and dating scene in and around Atlanta, and how there *was* a scene for just about anything an adult human could legally be into.

A few people swam in the rectangular lap pool or lounged in the serpentine curves of what everyone called The Chill Pond. Keith had to admit he was tempted. He knew without having to look it up that his family's farm could still get hit with frost for a couple more weeks, and the Illinois nights remained decidedly cool.

The balmy seventy-three degrees playing across his skin combined with not starting work for a few days to create quite the tropical vacation vibe.

Keith found an empty spot along a fence made of reclaimed train rails set at the perfect heights for leaning or sitting, still warm from the intense Southern sun. His view of both pools and the twinkling orange and blue lights of Atlanta's lovely dual skylines was just distracting enough that he could pretend he wasn't really waiting.

And hoping.

The smoky scent of grilling chicken and burgers with herbs fresh from the garden had his belly reminding him that he would soon require his own fuel after feeding and turning the soil in four big garden boxes. But the roiling heat that had built up as he'd spent the afternoon talking to Josh made him want to hold off for a while longer.

That one was going to be trouble, that restless inner warmth said. *Trouble,* loud and clear.

Josh had that deer-in-the-headlights look of a guy either in the middle of freaking out or swerving close to it. *Except* when he instead had a decidedly flirty and confident air, a near-sexual swagger in his luscious deep voice and smile, and in those incredible green eyes.

Oh yeah. Trouble for sure, and best avoided.

The rest of Keith hummed and whistled and smiled in blissful anticipation. Hoping the sweetest kind of trouble hit him hard and fast and deep.

That had always been when the most intense, memorable, and exciting relationships hit. When Keith wasn't expecting or looking, and a man or woman walked into his life who fit his current internal configuration perfectly. A few short hours with Josh made it clear he'd be a damn good fit right now.

Keith had the strangest feeling the fit might last a lot longer than right now. Josh might even be a person Keith could change and grow and shift *with* rather than breaking apart.

And because in Keith's life, timing was indeed everything, he wasn't the least bit surprised to look up right into Josh's dreamy eyes.

"We didn't do enough chores to be allowed into the pool with the big kids?"

Keith laughed, amazed at how fast the heat in his belly leapt into his heart. Josh's bed-head hair was calmer and a bit damp around the edges, just begging Keith's fingers to mess it up again. His black jeans and forest green shirt—no way he'd accidently chosen that color with those eyes—

showed off his strong shoulders and narrow waist to perfection.

"We must still be on probation," Keith said. "I think they do these mixers every couple of weeks, so we might get there next time."

He took a deep breath, and he could almost hear the steady metallic clack of a roller coaster getting to the top of the first huge, terrifying hill.

The start of the whole thrilling ride.

"I'm glad you came down, Josh. I wasn't sure you would."

CHAPTER 5

*J*osh smiled and took a sip of his beer, wondering if he looked as understood, as *seen*, as he felt. He'd spent a long few minutes staring into his closet, trying to imagine how he'd feel right this second. And how much worse he'd feel if he skipped the whole thing and stayed upstairs instead

"I wasn't sure either," he said, leaning against the thick metal fence beside Keith. "After you put me to work this afternoon, the temptation of lazing around and watching a bad movie hit pretty strong."

He risked a glance up into Keith's blue eyes, and Keith's half smile and a wink sent all of Josh's insides into a slow, delicious roll.

"Then I decided I'd rather hear more of your travel stories instead," Josh said. "See what I might be getting myself into by stepping out into the big scary world."

"That might take a while, but I get the feeling we've got plenty of time. I can tell you wherever I am never gets dull or boring. I make damn sure of that."

Josh turned and met Keith's gaze full on, relaxing into the warmth and curiosity and welcome he found there. The strong, clear feeling that while this new life would be unfamiliar and frightening sometimes—and he might indeed get hurt—the bold explorer hidden away inside all these years was wide awake and delighted to make his escape at long last.

And more than up for the challenge.

Josh didn't quite understand why the man beside him felt like such a natural piece of the puzzle. But he was ready to face his fear head-on and figure that out.

He scooted his hand closer on the warm metal and brushed his pinky against Keith's. He couldn't help but sigh when Keith looped one finger over his with a gentle squeeze.

"Then just start at the beginning," Josh said. "And tell me *everything*. I'll do my best to do the same. I think you may be right. We have plenty of time."

DIRK KNIGHT
THE CASE OF THE RUSTLED RANCH
JASON A. ADAMS
Author of Angel of Mercy and Moulin Rouge

PROLOGUE

Atlanta never sleeps.

From Roswell to Jonesboro, from Smyrna to Stone Mountain. The Big Peach hums and roars twenty-five hours a day. The city has seen its share of movie stars, moguls, and mobsters. Saints and sinners living, loving, and dying in the mosquito-filled swampy air of this global hub of humanity.

Most of the people living in The City of Trees are decent folk who mind their manners and do their jobs. But, as with any mixed barrel, sometimes a rotten apple gets down in the middle of things and causes a spreading blight of trouble.

That's when the good citizens of Atlanta call on Dirk Knight, Private Eye.

CHAPTER 1

The twenty-first of June. A Tuesday. 3:13 PM. Sodden heat blanketed the city like a sheepskin rug fresh from the washing machine. Dirk Knight turned the rusty box fan up another notch and moved it from the window to his desk. The stiff breeze blew his loosened tie over his shoulder, but his trusty gray fedora kept his hair in place.

His basement office wasn't comfortable, but beggars can't be choosers. A plain concrete floor went well with the cinderblock walls. A pair of threadbare curtains printed with faded flowers that once might have been yellow blocked off the gas furnace in one corner. Against the left-hand wall, the treadmill Doc Junkers had badgered him into buying now made a fine clothes-drying rack. The opposite wall had a flight of plank stairs with an unvarnished banister of two-by-fours leading up to the building's ground floor.

A vintage black Model 500 rotary phone perched on the desk, coiled in anticipation, waiting for the next call.

Dirk was a real private detective, but only had one case at the moment. A case of nerves.

Dark patches of moisture marked his armpits and spine. A sour taste of anxiety coated the back of his tongue. The waistband of his suit pants, bought when he'd been full of good intentions about diet and exercise, bit into his gut, reminding him he needed to clean off that damn treadmill one of these days. His thick fingers shook. He could smell himself, but no time for a shower.

Shit, he needed to get control. His old demon was riding his back, and he finally gave in.

The antique oak desk chair squealed like a scalded pig whenever he sat down. The only other chair, repurposed from his grandmother's kitchen, sat waiting patiently for a visitor. The flowery padding didn't really scream *detective's office*, but the price had been right.

The desk itself, a battered old teacher's model salvaged from the DeKalb County annual surplus sale, held the medicine he needed in the bottom drawer where most people would keep files.

Dirk rummaged past a dog-eared copy of Chandler's *The Big Sleep,* the cover nearly obscured by the duct tape holding his bible together.

Ah, there it was, right at the back.

He took the plastic bag and set it on the desk, staring. He should be stronger than this. He should stay to the straight and narrow.

To hell with it. Dirk deserved this.

He fished in the bag and drew out two miniature reesie cups. Only two. Dr. J. would just have to give him a pass

Today was a big day. His first client as a licensed detective. All the hours of online training, the five hundred bucks in licensing fees, all worth it. Twenty-eight years from cradle to credentials.

Dirk dug under the leather suspender strap on his left shoulder. In his IT days, he'd been a jeans and t-shirt kinda guy, but a gumshoe needed to dress the part. Black suit, black tie, white oxford shirt, black shoes polished to a high shine. And the fedora, of course.

His thin suspenders were part of the look, but mainly they served to keep his pants up. Belts didn't work for a guy with a belly wider than his ass.

He'd bought a London Fog trench coat to round things out, but it would probably be stuck decorating the coat tree as long as he stayed in Georgia. He'd shucked the suit jacket shortly after entering the office, and it had joined the rest of the treadmill wardrobe.

Dirk popped the reesies in his mouth, chewing and waiting for the knock at his door.

CHAPTER 2

*B*arbara Collins had a bad case of nerves.

She walked slowly up East Lake Road, carefully checking the house numbers. It seemed strange that a private eye's office would be in a house, but that's what the guy said.

She'd found his business card on the corkboard at the local Krispy Kreme. As a recent graduate of the Atlanta Culinary Institute, she didn't eat out much, except for donuts. There was something about a good donut; the yeasty aroma, the sweet sweet icing, the nutty flavor when fresh from floating down a river of grease, the way they seemed to melt against the tongue…

Some things were too dangerous to make at home. Every sinful bite meant fifteen extra minutes at the Y, but she had plenty of time.

She couldn't open her restaurant until she had

money, and for money she needed to market her products. She was waiting to hear back from several of the local health food stores and independent grocers. That stress had her in the Krispy Kreme more often than she'd like.

Barb had been scanning the flyers and notices while waiting for her half-dozen hots when she saw the little beige rectangle and thought why not? She definitely needed help, and the idea of hiring a private dick seemed pretty cool.

She finally found the place. A dark green Craftsman with black iron numbers on one of the porch pillars. 340 East Lake. The corner post had a hand-painted sign reading *Dirk Knight Detective Agency*, with an arrow pointing to a brick path around the side of the house.

Barb was starting to have second thoughts, but she had to do something. That little shit Maurice couldn't get away with selling *her* recipe. She had to get proof that he'd stolen her idea, and for that, she needed an investigator.

So, she'd pulled the card down and called the number. Dirk Knight himself answered. Secretary out sick, but please tell me what you need.

He'd sounded young, but professional. Almost like a character out of one of those black and white movies her dad loved so much.

A short flight of cement steps led down to a door with fresh paint the color of strawberry jam. The frosted glass bore gold lettering in the same hand-writing as the sign on the porch, announcing she had indeed located Dirk Knight's office.

She still had time. She could still turn around and go home, and stop fretting so much over Maurice and his recipe pilfering. The Internet was full of knock-off recipes for every famous edible out there, and those companies were still in business.

Still. This was her first foray into marketing her own goods, and she needed some signature some-thing to help her stand out in a city full of here-today, gone-tomorrow restaurants, diners, and food trucks.

Barb straightened up, squared her shoulders, got a good tight grip on her purse, and knocked.

CHAPTER 3

irk jerked awake, his chair falling backward as he tried to catch himself and failed, sprawling on the hard cement floor, catching his knee a hard crack on the unforgiving surface.

"One moment!" he yelled, grabbing the edge of the desk and hauling himself up. He eyed his jacket, decided it was still too hot, and instead quickly rolled his shirt sleeves up a couple of laps. He yanked his tie a little looser and tilted the fedora back on his head.

A quick check in his pocket mirror to make sure of the effect. A quick righting of his overturned chair. He winced at the shriek when he sat back down.

Dirk could see a female shadow through the window.

This was it. A real client. He puffed in his hand and sniffed. No halitosis, just peanut butter and chocolate.

He propped his shiny shoes on the desk, ankles crossed, leaning back with his hands locked behind his sweaty head.

"Come in," he said loudly.

The door opened, and *she* walked in.

Dirk tried not to stare, but it wasn't easy. She was a knockout. Five-ten, maybe six feet tall. Mid-twenties. Short mahogany hair curled across her brow and over her ears, flashing a few auburn highlights in the glow coming through the door. A pleasantly padded figure that made him forget all about the bruise on his knee. She'd been poured into a pair of yoga pants that clung to her curves like chocolate on a truffle. A forest green blouse with wide, lacy cuffs and a neckline lower than a politician's morals completed the outfit.

"Are you Mr. Knight?" she asked in a voice that dripped honey and promise.

"I am Dirk Knight, yes. And you must be Ms. Barbara Collins."

Dirk took his feet off the desk and stood, wiping his sweaty palm on his pants before holding it out to her, thinking how unfair it was that Philip Marlowe never sweated.

"Please, call me Barb," she said, taking his hand

in surprisingly firm grip. "I do hope you can help me, Mr. Knight."

"That's what I'm here for, ma'am. Please, have a seat. Coffee? Red Bull?" He caught sight of the candy bag still on the desk and felt his cheeks warm. "Um, chocolate?"

"No, but thank you, Mr. Knight." Barb sat in his granny's rickety kitchen chair, leaning forward, expectant.

"So tell me," Dirk said, sitting down. They both winced at the shriek. "What can a guy like me do for a dame like you?"

"Da— Ah, well…you see…" She fidgeted, her fingers curling around each other like mating octopuses. Octopi? Never mind.

"Just the facts, please."

Ms. Collins' eyes flicked back and forth. Dirk wondered if he should have showered.

"Here's the thing, Mr. Knight," she finally began. "I'm a chef. A *real* chef, not some jumped-up fry cook. I want to open my own restaurant, but I need to make some money first."

"Uh-huh. Go on," Dirk said, pulling a pocket notebook from his…pocket…and clicking a ball-point pen.

"I've been re-imagining classic sauces and condiments so I can market my own brand. But one of my ex-partners, Maurice Kadnes, stole my recipes, and is selling them at his own bistro."

"What sort of recipes?" Dangerous territory. Dirk's blood sugar was still low, and lunch was two hours in its grave.

"Vinaigrettes, aiolis, other sorts of dressings," she said. Her eyes burned bright as flashlights now. She sat up a little straighter, and Dirk thought a smile might be lurking around her mouth somewhere. She was definitely passionate about her stuff.

"What other sorts? I need all the details, Ms. Collins." He was trying for professional, but mainly he wanted to hear more about what made her light up like that.

"One especially. My personal favorite. It's my own take on a creamy buttermilk, garlic, and herb blend. Just a hint of sour cream and homemade mayonnaise make all the difference."

Dirk wiped a hand across the wet corner of his lips, disguising the move with a thoughtful chin rub.

"That sounds like Hidden Val—"

"No!" she snapped, slamming her palm on the desk with a sound like the starting gun at a college track meet. "It's *not* like that at all! What I make has no similarity to that powdered, processed, corporate devil dust!"

"Okay, okay," he said, raising his hands in surrender. "It's a totally different version. But tell me, Ms. Collins, why do you think he stole your recipes instead of just coming up with something similar on his own?"

"Because he has no imagination," she said, eyebrows pulling together over a perfect nose. "He used to be an accountant, and thinks he can run restaurants better than us true culinary artists."

"Any proof he's using your ideas?"

She slumped a little, and Dirk felt like a real shit for damping her fire.

"No, of course not. That's why I need you. But I've tasted his stuff, and I know my own when it's on my tongue."

Dirk was about to reply when the sound he'd been most afraid of split the quiet basement air.

"*JERRY!! Dinner's ready. Will your friend be joining us?*"

They both jumped.

"Who was that?" Barb asked, staring toward the door at the top of the stairs. "And who's Jerry?"

"Nothing. No one," Dirk said. His face was on fire. "I'll take the job, Ms. Collins. Tell me where to find this Maurice Kadnes's bistro, and I'll call you with a report once I check things out."

He stood and shuffled from foot to foot as his client scribbled an address in his notebook, then ushered her quickly to the door.

"Goodbye, Ms. Collins. Don't worry. I'm on the case."

CHAPTER 4

*B*arb left the detective's office, if you could call it that. She wasn't exactly brimming with confidence in his abilities, but he seemed eager.

She wondered if she should have told him more about Maurice and his hobbies.

Nah. Dirk—that is, Mr. Knight—could handle himself. Maurice would take one look at Di—Mr. Knight's large frame and confident smile, and faint.

Her tired old Civic wheezed and shuddered through the evening traffic as she made her slow way back to her utilitarian hovel of an apartment. Her family was on her to get a real job, so she could get a real place to live.

Screw that. She had dreams, dammit!

Dirk, Mr. Knight, was kinda cute.

Now where had that come from? Sure, he had that dark red hair that magically curled itself and a scatter of *adorable* freckles across his nose and cheeks. Like a little Irish cherub. He was big enough that a girl could curl up and lose herself in his…

Stop it, Barb.

She needed him to make Maurice stop his shenanigans, not to fill her lonely evenings.

She stopped at the farmer's market for more organic, grass-fed buttermilk. The buttermilk was the real key to her signature dressing, but she always talked more about the other ingredients to keep the secret.

Her dressing would pay for the restaurant and more once she got it in the stores. She was sure of it.

Twenty minutes later, Barb left the market. She threw bags full of buttermilk, dill, and the rest of the necessary raw materials in the Honda's back seat, making sure not to break the unlabeled jar of MSG that was her other secret ingredient.

No one needed to know about *that*, surely.

She'd overheard two tasteless soccer moms carrying on about that *fabulous* new café, with that *fabulous* young chef Maurice, who made such *fabulous* salads.

Barb's eyes prickled, and she blinked rapidly,

furious with herself. She wasn't about to give that… that…*wannabe* the satisfaction, even if the little twerp couldn't see her.

God, she needed Krispy Kreme.

CHAPTER 5

he woke the next morning with a new determination which helped take her mind off her aching tummy. She needed to take Dirk a sample of her best dressing. Just so he could compare it with whatever he found at Maurice's of course.

The red ribbon and hand-written label, *For my favorite Private Eye*...well, that was just being polite.

Barb called Dirk's number. Mr. Knight's number. The detective office. She couldn't keep her head straight this morning. Must be after-shocks from several glazed donuts. And two cream-filled.

He answered on the third ring.

"Dirk Knight, Private Eye," said her detective.

She smiled, glad to hear his voice.

"Mr. Knight? This is Barb. Barbara Collins. You agreed to look into my problem?"

"Um, yeah," he said. He sounded odd, somehow. Slurred. She looked at her watch. Surely he wasn't drinking at ten in the morning.

"So I had a couple of things I wanted to show you. If it's not too much trouble, could I come by? I can be there in half an hour."

A long pause greeted this.

"Mr. Knight?"

Did he not want to see her? Could he tell how hard she was gripping her cell phone? She couldn't afford to replace another cracked phone.

"Yeah. Yes, of course. Come by, but in an hour instead of half. And Ms. Collins, I have some things to tell you, as well."

The line went dead. Barb stared at her phone. Dirk seemed upset. Was he upset with her? Or was it something else? Maybe she'd interrupted him with his girlfriend? That voice from up the stairs?

Never mind. What Mr. Knight did on his own time was none of her business.

She packed the sample bottle in her purse. She thought about losing the ribbon, but decided to keep it. It was just a friendly gift. Piece of evidence. Whatever. Nothing for anyone to get jealous over.

The drive back to Mr. Knight's office seemed to take forever. Barb alternated between worry at what she might've done wrong, what the detective had to tell her, who that woman was, who Jerry was for that matter.

She finally parked on the street outside Mr. Knight's bungalow and walked around to his office. A quick dab of vanilla on her wrists, just in case she'd gotten sweaty or something, and she knocked.

"Come in."

It was Dirk's voice, but she again heard the wrongness. Maybe he was sick? Barb pushed the door open and stepped into the office.

And sucked in a breath, hands jumping to her mouth.

Dirk sat at his desk like yesterday, but that was the only thing the same.

His hat was gone. His hair, although damp from a shower or bath, stuck out all over the place. His lips puffed out, but not in any kind of alluring way. His right cheekbone was split, and his right eye looked like a plum pudding baked at 400 instead of 350.

Wasn't Maurice left-handed?

"Hello, Ms. Collins. Forget to tell me your perp is a double black belt in Tae Kwon Do?"

"Oh my goodness, I'm so sorry!" she said through her hands. "What happened? I hate Maurice, but I never thought he'd attack anyone! You poor thing!"

She rushed around the desk and gave him a hug, loosening up when he hissed. She felt terrible. No one was supposed to get mauled over salad dressing.

Food was supposed to make people happy!

"It's okay," Dirk said, patting her arm. "I'm fine, really. Just a little tenderized."

At least he didn't tell her to let go.

"Why don't you sit down, and I'll tell you what I've got."

CHAPTER 6

Dirk really didn't want to do this.

When Barb called, he'd been equal parts ashamed and happy. Happy because he really wanted to see her face, client or not, and ashamed at what he needed to tell her. The hug made it easier. At least he'd have that, if not any fee.

Once she'd let him loose and sat down, he sighed and ran his hands—carefully—through his hair.

"So I checked into copyright and trademark law. It seems there's no protection for recipes, since lists of ingredients and steps are considered factual, not artistic."

"But that's not fair!" Barb said. Now she looked angry.

"Look, there's no way to prove that you're the only one who ever combined those ingredients in that way," he said, wishing he could make this easier. "Anyway, once I figured out we...*you* couldn't go after Maurice on copyright grounds, I went to try and talk him into doing the right thing."

"If you look like this, how bad is he?" she asked, leaning forward. Her eyes sparkled, and her moist lips parted slightly.

Dirk saw all that before he looked down at the desk. Someone had carved *JK luvs HP* under where the teacher's blotter probably once sat. Great detective work on his part, unearthing something like that.

"He's just fine and dandy. I never laid a hand on him." He hated the way his voice had shrunk.

Who the hell had he been kidding, anyway?

"I might as well tell you the truth," he said, still not looking at his silent client. "I'm no detective. I mean, I got my PI license, but that was just classroom work and a multiple-choice test. I'm just a computer geek with delusions of grandeur who got downsized when my last company reorganized. I wanted to do something exciting, and I thought I could be like Marlowe and Hammer and Bogart. I'm sorry, Ms. Collins. You hired a phony." He wiped his sleeve across his eyes and spun in his chair to face the wall.

She didn't say anything for a minute. Then, "But you have an office, and a license. You even know how to research a case, right? I mean, you found out about the copyright stuff."

"That wasn't anything but a Google search," he said past the lump in his throat. "I'm a fraud. You asked who Jerry is? *I'm* Jerry. Jerry Farnsworth. That was my mom calling me to supper the other day. I wanted to be Dirk Knight because Dirk Knight is a gritty, hard-boiled gumshoe, not a loser unemployed computer tech like Jerry Farnsworth who lives with his mother. Some great detective, huh?"

CHAPTER 7

arb's heart ached for Dirk. Jerry. She knew how he must feel.

"If you're a fraud, then so am I," she said, standing and walking around the desk to put a hand on his meaty shoulder.

"Two years ago, I was a line cook at Applebee's. I thought I was good enough to go to culinary school, and then I thought I was good enough to get rich selling salad dressing, of all things. I hired you because I thought Maurice was stealing my ideas, but I might as well call myself Mrs. Wishbone."

She hated the way his shoulders shook, but he made no noise.

What happened between this insecure guy and the sneaky but mostly harmless Maurice? Sure, he worked out at a dojo three days a week, but he'd always said that was it, a workout. He didn't even compete in the tournaments.

"Why did Maurice attack you, Jerry?"

"Self-defense," he muttered. "I attacked him, not the other way around."

"Why on earth—"

"Because he said…he called you…Never mind. He made me angry, and I took a swing at him."

He'd been mad enough to assault a stranger because of something Maurice said about her? Warm flutters rippled through her abdomen.

"Anyway, I'm sorry I can't do anything for you," he said. "No charge, since I didn't accomplish anything."

"That's okay," Barb said. She noticed her hand was still on his shoulder. Her other hand wanted to join it. "Oh, wait. I do have something for you."

Barb reached around and got the dressing bottle out of her purse. She turned the squeaky desk chair until he was facing her, then put her fingers under his chin and tilted his face up until he was looking at her.

"Jerry, I'm actually very proud of you," she said. "You risked everything to chase your dream, and that's worth a lot. I don't *have* a lot, unfortunately, but I do have this."

She handed the ribboned bottle to him. He took it and pulled the stopper, tilted the white cream onto a finger, and tasted it. His eyes went wide, and he smiled.

"That's amazing, Barb! I mean, Ms. Collins. The best I've ever tasted!"

"Thank you. You can have all you want, since I haven't been able to sell any. Please promise me you won't give up on Dirk Knight just yet. Give him a year or two to work his kinks out."

To her surprise, he gave her a bashful smile and opened a drawer in the ugly old desk.

"That reminds me. I have something for you too," he said, taking a shiny sheet of plastic from the drawer.

"I felt bad about not being able to help, so I got hold of a friend of mine who does graphic design for a packaging company." He held the sheet behind his back, still smiling.

"You're right, Barb. Salad dressings are a dime a dozen. Good as yours is, taste doesn't sell stuff like that, the label does. What you need is something clever that'll grab people's eye. If you can get a chuckle out of them, even better."

"Tada!" he said, holding the sheet up to her face with a flourish.

"Oh my God, I love it!" Barb said, clapping her hands and bouncing like a little kid.

The sheet was a pink label, covered with bright daisies. Fifties-style script read, "Barbie's Dream Ranch."

"I can get as many labels as you can get full bottles," he said. "Don't give up on *your* dream either, Barb."

She took his hands in hers and pulled him to his feet.

"Tell you what, big boy. I'll stick to mine if you stick to yours."

She surprised them both by planting her lips on his for far longer than a kiss between new friends required.

"I think we should celebrate Dirk Knight's Detective Agency and Barbie's Dream Ranch," she said when they finally broke apart. "How does a lunch date sound?"

"Great!" Dirk said. "Anything but salad."

They both laughed, and it struck Barb how natural it felt to hold this man's hands and laugh with him.

"Just let me change out of this ridiculous suit," he said. "Be thinking about where you want to go. It's my treat."

"Have you tried Krispy Kreme's Reese's donuts?" she asked, squeezing his hands. "And don't forget your fedora, *Dirk*."

THE REAL *Treasure* IN CAIRO

KARI KILGORE

For Jason

Who knows why

CHAPTER 1

The rusty metal slat door of the storage pod rattled up with a squeal, setting April Owens's teeth on edge. Her wavy brown hair felt like a damp wool scarf against her neck, even though the September afternoon was fairly cool for Cairo, Illinois.

Properly pronounced *Kay*-row with the twist of local dialect, not at all like the desert city in Egypt. Not that anyone would ever mistake this part of the country for any kind of desert.

Even compared to typical St. Louis late summer weather, eighty-five degrees with well over ninety percent humidity was incredibly sticky and miserable.

The pea-soup thick air had long since had its way with the ball bearings in the door's frame. Or else—like so many other things in and around Cairo—no one had tended to it for far too long.

The vast storage complex sat on the Ohio River side, row after endless row of cinderblocks painted brown a long time ago. The paint was peeling off the same way the faded asphalt had cracked and heaved after years of not much attention. Weeds sprouted around the edges of each set of buildings, along the deeper cracks in the pavement, and even on the roof in a few places.

A thick, dusty smell carried on chilly air utterly at odds with the damp all around rolled out of the storage unit. April took a step back and covered her nose, trying to fight off a sneezing fit. Between congestion from mold and mildew and sneezes from the dust, she'd be a disgusting mess before she ever got started digging through her Uncle Jefferson's things.

The string-bean woman beside her didn't seem to notice the dust or heat or anything else. Mrs. Simms just stared straight ahead with faded gray eyes, rolling a chewed wooden matchstick from one corner of her mouth to the other. At least the striking end was outside.

The crisscrossing but not very deep lines on her face and coarse steel gray hair on her head left April with no idea how old she actually was.

But she'd bet Mrs. Simms remembered much better days in Cairo.

Better than even the late Eighties visits April recalled so fondly, from back before she was quite a teenager.

She switched on the flashlight Mrs. Simms had given her back at the depressing and run-down office, then stepped back again. Rather than taking up half the width of the building like she expected, leaving a wall on the opposite side attached to a separate unit, the space stretched all the way across the building. Easily thirty feet deep, and a good twenty across.

And every single inch jammed full of *stuff*.

April saw couches, mattresses, tables and chairs, shelves full of books, even appliances that had to be a hundred years old or more. She knew there would be clocks and photos and little figurines and dolls and baseball cards and who knew what else tucked away and out of sight.

Everyone in the family remembered Uncle Jefferson being a terrible packrat. He'd saved everything that ever passed through his hands or his house that he could possibly convince himself wasn't garbage. Anything "someone could get some good use out of someday."

Now that April stood face-to-face with what she'd just landed in the middle of, her resolution to sort through it all and figure out what was worth donating faltered. Badly.

"I only have two weeks to go through all of this?" April said, barely louder than a whisper.

Mrs. Simms barked out harsh laughter.

"*This*? Didn't they tell you about the other two units?"

April turned her head slowly and stared at Mrs. Simms.

"Three? There are three? All like this?"

Mrs. Simms nodded, and April was sure she saw a smile lurking on the hateful woman's face.

"I'd say they're stacked up worse. Been sitting here for more than ten years. Contract said I had to keep the A/C on, Damp Rid filled up all around them, but not a thing more than that. When this place shuts down, all this crap goes with it. Into the rivers for all I care. Hope you got someone to help you. And can take that much time off work."

April drew in a shuddering breath, then regretted when she finally sneezed, catching it against her shoulder just in time.

"Well, I have the time. I teach at Wash U up in St. Louis, so I'm off for the summer. I guess you could say I have help. My sister's coming in from Ohio. And some museum curator keeps calling. I mean, I asked around back in St. Louis when I heard about this, she didn't just call out of nowhere. She wants to take a look at what's here."

Mrs. Simms snorted, but she did hand April a

clean tissue. April had no idea where it had come from, but she was grateful.

"I'd say you want to let that curator gal take everything she will and dump the rest. A lot of folks are just forfeiting their last few months' rent so we'll haul it off. Never even bother to peek inside the doors. Want to see the other two units?"

April shook her head, trying to stand up tall with her shoulders back. Maybe if she pretended she had the strength of ten women, she might be able to get through this.

She'd need at least that much strength just to get through more than a couple of hours with her sister.

"Not right now, Mrs. Simms, thank you. Maybe tomorrow. I'll make my phone calls and we'll get started then."

CHAPTER 2

*M*ichele Brankowski parked beside the twelfth row of identically decrepit storage units, hoping the woman she was supposed to meet would be on time. From the looks of the rusty fences, crumbling roads, and peeling paint on the units, the only sensible thing might be to bulldoze the whole thing into a big hole it the ground.

Strange as it might seem to others, she much preferred to evaluate furniture or appliances or collectibles still inside the houses. Even if people had passed away there. She found it much more creepy and disturbing to look at the contents that made a house a home after they were yanked out and jammed into a space they were never meant for. Where no one cared enough to keep them, arrange them, or even enough to simply pass them along or throw them away.

Like seeing a child's precious stuffed animal abandoned in a mud puddle, everything in a storage unit seemed so sad and defeated.

She walked toward unit number 1276, thankful she'd wrangled her thick red hair into a braid before leaving St. Louis that morning. She'd never quite managed to prepare herself for leaving from one of the most humid cities in the country and arriving somewhere even more swampy less than three hours later.

Her t-shirt and jeans immediately got way too cozy with her skin, but trying to pluck the damp fabric away was useless.

As much as Michele hated the way Cairo had declined, even in her lifetime, she was always relieved to have a chance to save some small part.

Once a thriving transportation hub between the mighty Mississippi and Ohio rivers, the city lingered on now as almost a ghost town. So much history—some of it deeply disturbing—and so much of it lost to human economic and population decline rather than nature's raging floods.

About thirty feet ahead of her, a pile of black plastic bags in the middle of the weedy roadway marked what had to be her destination. Another bag came sailing out, followed by a huge sneeze and an impressive volley of very naughty words indeed.

Michelle smiled at the creative combinations. She respected a fellow artist working in one of her favorite mediums.

"Hello?" she called, not wanting the next load to land on her head. "Ms. Owens?"

A head with red cheeks and an unruly halo of brown hair popped out, followed by another string of profanities Michele was sure she wasn't supposed to hear.

"You're Ms. Brankowski? The curator?"

Michele closed the distance between them and held out her hand. The whole woman finally appeared, her perfectly curvy figure clad in ripped jeans and a t-shirt that might have been black about ten years ago. Back in the days when Michele couldn't yet imagine the comfortable solidity and confidence of her mid-forties.

"I'm the curator," she said, "but please call me Michele. Thank you so much for inviting me down to take a look. I know these kinds of family things can be rough to deal with."

"Oh, you'll see rough. Just wait 'til my sister gets here. And call me April. I don't know how much you'll find worth keeping in there, assuming we can even *get* to it all."

April rolled her wide brown eyes, and her smile didn't look exactly happy. Her full red lips were a little too pressed together for happy.

When Michele looked inside the unit, her own smile faltered.

They weren't quite into typical hoarder territory here. No towers of newspapers or broken plates or collections of empty milk jugs or any of the other heartbreaking signs of *that* challenge Michele had seen.

But April's Uncle Jefferson had apparently been a world-class packrat.

"Wow," she said under her breath. "We've got our work cut out for us."

April laughed with a bit of an uncomfortable edge underneath.

"I don't suppose you knew there are three of these, all just as full?"

Michele stepped forward, peering as far as she could into the cavernous storage unit. She spotted a white enamel gleam that looked promising, and a couple of cabinets that would be pure joy if their wavy glass fronts were still intact.

"No, I knew as much as you did," she said. "What are you throwing out?"

April pulled her spectacular waves of hair back with both hands, but when she let go it popped right back out into the humidified halo.

"I found a couple of chest-of-drawers full of socks and underwear. I think whoever cleaned out the house just brought them over here without even looking inside. So now it's my...my freaking problem."

Michele laughed and touched April's shoulder.

"*Our* problem. Like I said over the phone, I'm certain we'll find some wonderful things no matter how it looks right now. And the last thing you need to worry about with me is swearing. If we spend any amount of time together, you'll be surprised when you *don't* hear me let it fly."

April grinned and laughed for real this time.

"That's a relief. Because I think this is going to be an all-day-swearing kind of job."

CHAPTER 3

April tried to keep herself from checking her watch every few minutes, but it got harder as the morning wore on toward afternoon. She expected Fran to be a couple of hours late, of course, especially when she wasn't going to be the center of a bunch of people's attention.

But stretching a promise to be there by eight to pushing noon without even a phone call or text was still a bit much.

On the other hand, April had no doubt in her mind that the work was going exponentially faster without her older sister's interference and never-ending stream of oh-so-precious advice.

Er, her *help*.

And because Michele actually *did* help so much, and with a hell of a lot more than sorting and moving Uncle Jefferson's things, the hours and the work were flying by.

They'd made quite a bit more headway than she possibly could have imagined standing next to sour Mrs. Simms yesterday. The piles outside had been shifted into two empty units across the roadway: one for landfill or recycling-bound, another for local donation if possible. The move was to keep the roadway clear, to create a bit of walking room, and just in case the saturated air tipped over from can't-possibly-hold-one-more-drop to a roaring downpour.

Blue skies and fluffy white clouds overhead made that seem unlikely, but the hopes of a woman drowning because she didn't have gills seemed eternal.

Several pieces of furniture too large too move still dotted the front of her uncle's unit—along with the things Michele was interested in—but they'd almost reached the halfway point in their inventory and clearing. Michele had marked a surprising number of big and small items for various museums she scouted for.

A tiny little gas range with a black top and a miniature white oven door that said "New Process." A barely shoulder-high refrigerator with curved edges and a huge round compressor on top. A couple of iron bedframes painted white. And a strange collection of oddly shaped lamps that

Michele said were old TV-top lamps, thought to protect viewers' eyes in the early days.

April's favorite was a sleek black panther with green glass eyes that she was considering keeping for herself.

Besides all that knowledge and muscle and help with decision-making, April was enjoying Michele's conversation and company. She couldn't remember the last time she'd laughed so much or felt so comfortable with someone she'd just met.

Probably never, if she was being honest.

The rosy flush in Michele's pale cheeks and that gorgeous red braid down her back or falling across her shoulder sure didn't hurt.

"Where are you taking all these things?" April said, watching Michele sort a bunch of kitchen stuff into a box on top of the little range.

"All kinds of communities are setting up nice history museums, not just big cities any more. It's a bit dusty in here, but almost everything is in great shape. I'd almost use this sifter in my kitchen at home. Almost."

Michele held up what looked like a cake pan, but it was brown with white speckles and had holes in the bottom.

"Towns like Cairo are full of great finds like this, if only the museums can get to them in time. Even if they don't need big things like the refrigerator, little touches like the shaving brush and cup or even the towering ashtray over there can make a big difference in how the museum *feels*."

April couldn't hold back her smile at Michele's perfect pronunciation. *Kay*-row. She looked at the almost waist-high gold-toned thing in the corner, wide on the bottom, narrow in the middle, with a flattened dome on top.

"*Ashtray*? I swear to you I thought that thing was a model of a UFO."

Their sweet shared giggling fit was interrupted by a sharp, purposeful, two-note throat clearing from just outside the storage unit.

April didn't even have to turn around to know who had finally arrived.

"I see things are progressing at the expected snail's pace."

April raised her eyebrows at Michele, then turned to greet her sister. She didn't bother getting up from where she knelt on an old couch cushion.

"Hi Fran. Traffic bad between here and Ohio?"

Frances Elaine Owens McClintock stood just outside the entrance in all her usual perfectly manicured and coiffured glory. In fact, she wore what had to be a designer white linen pantsuit, pale blue silk blouse, and spotless white high heels to go along with a swirling mass of expertly (and expensively) blonded hair.

Perfect for grubbing through a dusty storage unit on a hot, especially moist day.

"Traffic was dreadful, since you asked," Fran said. "I really should have flown."

"That's what I said when I talked to you about this a couple of weeks ago. Michele Brankowski, this is my sister Fran. Fran, Michele is the museum curator I told you about."

April was secretly pleased when Michele stayed where she was, deep in the storage unit dust and clutter, rather than approaching as Fran so clearly expected.

"Nice to meet you, Fran."

Fran looked down at the concrete floor, now covered with two sets of dusty footprints. She spoke without looking up.

"Likewise, Ms. Brankowski. A curator for what *sort* of museum? Up in St. Louis I presume?"

"Sometimes," Michele said, gathering up a stack of ancient cookbooks. "Mostly I scout for smaller museums across the country and into Canada. Your uncle's things are quite a treasure trove."

"I'm certain they are," Fran said. "Your *friend* isn't here to help you, April?"

April closed her eyes, wishing she could disappear Fran or herself. April and the *friend* Fran couldn't bring herself to mention by name had lived together for four years.

The hell of it was April was absolutely certain Fran had no trouble with her ex being a woman.

Fran had no trouble with April having an ex.

Fran had never expressed anything but barely concealed pleasure when April's relationships passed themselves into history.

As it turned out, not everyone found their perfect tight-assed match, got married straight out of college, and stayed that way. Then proceeded to gloat about it for the next two decades.

"Diane hasn't been around for about a year now, Fran. You know that. You drove all the way from Columbus in that outfit? Got something to change into?"

Fran laughed and examined her French manicure.

"Of *course* I didn't drive all the way from Columbus today, April. I stayed in Paducah overnight. I have clothes in the car. But I'm sure we can find someone to hire to take care of all this."

Michele's incredulous gaze met April's, and April knew they were thinking exactly the same thing.

April had already *found* someone to take care of this. All of this.

And Paducah was barely one hour away.

April got to her feet and brushed her dusty hands on her already dusty jeans.

"I'm sorry, but excuse me, Michele. I need to have a word with my sister."

CHAPTER 4

$\mathcal{M}$ichelle set the collection of absolutely beautiful antique cook-books on top of the gorgeous gas stove. Probably from around 1915, that stove, and in incredibly good condition.

She headed back into the storage unit, doing her best not to listen or even glance out at April dealing with her nightmare of a sister.

Michele knew the type too well after years of these family situations.

She'd be willing to bet a year's worth of her pay from all the museums she worked with that April's sister Fran kept herself away from all the difficult parts. No worries about growing medical trouble with older relatives, or long-term care facilities, or agonizing choices about the eventual end of life.

No, Fran fit the sadly typical stereotype of the

sibling who found a lot to complain about, no matter what the person doing all the work managed to work out.

And then expected to swoop in and gather up credit and sympathy in the end, not to mention any financial rewards that might come along.

From overstuffed storage units, for example.

As melancholy as dying cities like Cairo made her feel, sometimes they were the source of amazing discoveries like these units promised to be. Wealthy and prosperous in the late Nineteenth and early Twentieth centuries, when so many areas of household necessities were at their stylistic peak as far as she was concerned.

Everything from sofas to ovens to hand mirrors and even telephones were curvy and colorful and a real pleasure to look at. (kind of like April)

The sad fact of the slow decline might even have helped preserve all these treasures.

People kept things a bit longer. Maintained them more carefully. They were often reluctant to part with the older models even when they could afford new.

The sharp tone of raised voices sent her deeper into the tour of Midwestern domestic history all around her.

After a few delightful hours of combing through these treasures—and in April's even more delightful company—Michele had Uncle Jefferson pegged as a man who'd come from a wealthy Cairo family and did well for himself as a young man. But as rail, river, and finally automobile traffic decisions cut off the city's lifeblood, he'd collected what he could in his huge rambling house.

Partly because of his experience and memories of the Great Depression, certainly. But Michele suspected he'd also wanted to keep back what he could for his family or anyone else who might be in need. That matched with the stories April told of his generosity.

The same generosity Michele saw in April wanting to donate as much as she could not only to the museums, but to the local community.

Michele had long since lost track of how many families she'd helped through kind of transition. And she knew very well the dangers of getting involved with clients.

But something about April had her willing—maybe even eager—to lower a bit of her customary armor.

April didn't see this as a junk pile or a massive windfall they could churn out on eBay or through some overhyped private auction. She took a clear-eyed view Michele rarely saw in people sorting through the possessions and collections of their loved ones' lives. A view firmly centered in reality.

That and everything else about April made her a woman Michele very much wanted to spend more time with. A woman she hoped to get to know a whole lot better.

Unfortunately, it sounded like Fran did *not* share that clear-eyed view with her sister, or much of anything else.

CHAPTER 5

April crossed her sweaty arms and continued to shake her head.

Fran stared back at her, sweat beading unattractively through the makeup above her upper lip. Or at least April thought Fran was staring. It was impossible to tell through those massive, dark sunglasses.

No.

She was not going to give in to Fran the way she had so many times over the years.

Sometimes because Fran was so relentless that April finally gave up.

Sometimes because April flat-out didn't want to hear any more.

But neither of those methods would work.

Not today.

Not about this.

"I don't understand why you're being so obstinate, April. I can have someone here the day after tomorrow. Proper movers who will load up all three of these units in a day. Then we'll get it to St. Louis or Chicago or wherever we need to for a proper appraisal. That's the only thing that makes sense."

"It might make sense to you, Fran. But you're not the only person here. And you're not even the executor, remember? *I* am. I asked you to come so you could see if you wanted to keep anything for yourself. It certainly wasn't because I expected you to help move things. I also didn't ask *you* to charge in and try to change everything *I* already decided."

Fran blotted just under her nose with a tissue, but sweat now trickled out of her hair and down her temples.

"There's simply no reason for me to move anything. Not when the whole lot needs to be transported at once. You can't seriously be thinking of giving all of this away to strangers."

April took a deep breath, wishing she was still smelling Michele's clean, honest sweat rather than Fran's overpowering floral perfume. If she were, her muscles would still be weary from a long morning, but they wouldn't be so tense and knotted up that she felt like a vibrating live wire.

Something about being with Michele made April feel like she'd never be tense again.

"I told you what I wanted to do when I called

you. How I wanted to handle the estate that Uncle Jefferson trusted to *me*, how this would make him happy. You didn't say a word about it then."

"Well, I'm saying it now. It would be a shame for all of Uncle Jefferson's things he loved so much to disappear into a bunch of third-rate small town museums."

"No, Fran. It would be a shame for all of them to end up sold for a fortune and no one ever seeing them again. He never would have wanted that. Never."

Fran blotted again, but saving her makeup job was a lost cause already.

"It's because of that woman, isn't it? She seems like your type. For as long as it lasts *this* time, anyway."

All at once, something in April's head shifted. Her mind's eye, and the even more important senses in her heart, slipped into perfect focus.

April smiled. And she didn't mind one bit when Fran drew back with a frown.

"You know what?" April said. "This is one hundred percent because of Uncle Jefferson, but I doubt you'd understand that if I stood here and explained it until they did dump all his things into the rivers. But you're right about one thing. Michele *is* my type. Very much so."

April stepped away and turned back toward the storage unit.

"If you want to keep anything, you need to speak up now, Fran. But I'm going to handle this *my* way, and that's the end of it. Uncle Jefferson was obviously right to trust me instead of you. Once I'm finished here, I won't listen to another word from you about it. Or anything else, to tell you the honest truth."

Fran's mouth dropped open, and she yanked off her sunglasses, dragging even more of the makeup off with them. Her narrowed eyes showed more ravages of the damp heat, with wide creases in the tasteful smoke-gray eyeshadow and a rather racoon-like ring of melting eyeliner.

"*What* did you just say to me? You think after everything I've done for you and this family that you'll just shove me aside and carry on about your merry way? You'll botch this just like you have the rest of your miserable little life!"

April closed the space between them before she realized she was going to, standing close enough to catch the stink of sweat under Fran's perfume.

Instead of the clammy, leaden feeling in her gut and around her heart when she'd tried to disagree with Fran in the past, a soaring, trembling excitement surged through her. Like lightning striking close enough to leave her eyes dazzled and her hair standing on end.

"My life has been going perfectly well without your interference, Fran, and apparently without you even noticing. Not that you're ever going to bother paying attention to anything that doesn't point back to glorious you in the end. Believe it or not, *all* of us get along better without you and your precious advice. But listening to you drone on over the phone is a hell of a lot easier than having to deal with you face to face."

Fran took a step back, wide-eyed with her cheeks and neck blotchy red.

"If you don't feel the need to *deal with me*, April, then I'll take myself right back home and out of your life. As soon as I have a look for myself to make sure you and your new little *friend* aren't hoarding anything truly valuable for yourselves."

She jammed her sunglasses back on and drew herself up.

"I might just have a word with this Michele myself, let her know exactly what she's getting into with the likes of you. Then we'll see how *interested* she is."

April threw back her head and laughed, loud and free and wonderful. An outburst of pure joy as she shed decades of tension, held too close and deep inside as she endured far too much of Fran's "advice."

Something she'd never do again after today.

"Knock yourself out, Fran. I'll even send the delightful Mrs. Simms over to keep you company and show you the other two units that are jammed just as full as this one. As for Michele, I'm taking her to lunch right now. I'll leave it up to her whether she wants to talk to you or not. But I've listened to my last of your advice."

April stepped back, finally removing herself from a lifelong trap that had never suited her.

"And even if she's not interested in me, or if it doesn't work out? It will still be worth trying. I'm not about to fossilize myself at twenty-two years old, or thirty-two, or forty-two. I'm honestly sorry that you did."

April walked away, not bothering to see if Fran was following her.

Michele was heading out from the back with an armful of glass bowls, all brushed clean and sparkling iridescent amber and beautiful patterns. She looked up at April with a cautious smile.

"Everything going okay out there?"

"Everything is going great. Fantastic, to tell you the truth." April took the bowls, set them down carefully, and grabbed both of Michele's hands.

"Listen, Michele, we've worked our asses off out here. I don't know about you, but I'm hot and thirsty and starving. Let me take you out to lunch? It might not be any fancy place or gourmet food today. But I hope to make that up to you later if you're interested. If you'll let me, and you can still stand the sight of me after days cooped up here with Uncle Jefferson's things."

Michele's eyebrows drew down, and she frowned a tiny bit.

"Trouble can so easily flare up with family at times like this. I did everything I could to keep from listening, but that sure sounded like trouble. I don't want to come between you and your sister."

April grinned and shook her head.

"That wasn't trouble you heard. Not new trouble, anyway. That was me finally standing up to her, something I should have done years ago. What you heard was *good*, and long overdue. Everything gets better from here."

Michele grinned back and squeezed April's hands.

"I told you we might find some real treasure here in Cairo. I was right about your Uncle Jefferson's things. But I'm starting to think the *real* treasure is you, April."

The two of them walked out into the sunshine hand in hand, right past a furious but silent Fran.

Toward whatever came next, together.

FOR THE LOVE OF
Snarla Jane

JASON A. ADAMS

For Bella, our own Snarla Jane.

CHAPTER 1

ill Jackson woke to the lovely sounds of thumps, grunts, and swearing from next door.

Great. The new neighbor must be moving in.

Groaning, he pulled a down pillow over his head and tried to go back to sleep. Nothing doing. If anything, the elephants over in #3 just stepped up the pace.

He could sleep through the thunder of fighter jets from the base across the road, and the constant traffic on Nellis Boulevard had become nothing more than white noise since he'd moved in a year ago.

But people? People woke him up every time.

He cracked his lids, checked the clock. 5:38 PM. Probably still eighty outside. The October sun would be going down soon, but he still had two hours of sleep coming, dammit!

But, normal people and the normal hours they kept often dragged him from the blissful land of Tempurpedia. Bill sighed, rubbed his eyes, and flipped on the bedside lamp.

He swung his legs over the side. Put his feet on the cool linoleum. Scratched his belly hair. Yawned until his jaws popped. Grimaced as the yawn pulled his morning breath back down.

Slowly, the cobwebs began to blow away. The sunny yellow floor, a refugee from someone's Harvest Gold nightmare, reflected lamplight up into the bedroom where it was immediately absorbed by the equally horrific faux-walnut paneling.

Gotta love mid-century-modern two-up-and-two-down dingbat apartments. Chock plumb full of enough kitsch and nostalgia to make a guy puke. Especially after the owner pulled all the stops on remodeling with period décor.

But the place was cheap, close to a bus line, and *usually* fairly quiet. For Las Vegas, anyway.

Unfortunately, all the stucco on the outside covered walls not much thicker than the formalde-hyde-factory paneling inside.

Bill knew he'd miss having an empty apartment next door. And the peace and quiet that went with it. The last neighbors had been pretty quiet, at least until their teenagers started bringing dates home. Or got brought home by the cops. Ugh.

Working night shift at the Meadowville Data Center brought good pay, and it might be time to shunt some of that pay toward a new place. Maybe an actual house, instead of another apartment.

Once the albatross of student loan debt was paid off, of course.

Ah well. Might as well accept the situation and check the new next-door out.

Did he hear a dog? That would be just friggin' perfect.

He had no problem with dogs in principle, but had no desire to interact with one of the hairy, smelly beasts. Maybe this one was with a friend or relative. A guy could hope, right? I mean, surely Manny Ortega, the building owner-slash-super, wouldn't let a dog in one of his precious apartments.

Bill picked up his phone, tapped the appropriate taps, and started looking for clothes that wouldn't scream "I might be night shift or I might be a serial killer." In the kitchen his bluetooth coffee maker began roasting and grinding the magical beans.

CHAPTER 2

Trisha Macintyre really, *really* wanted a shower.

She'd spent the afternoon trying to direct three hulking brutes—all of whom were badly in need of some quality time with a shower themselves—who seemed determined to give her a heart attack as they slung her meager possessions from the moving van, up the stairs, and into her new apartment. She was hot, parched, and ready for a nap.

The harsh chemical odors of new wood paneling, floor glue, and latex paint promised to send her to bed with an extra pain pill, but hopefully the open windows and ceiling fans would clear the worst of it out for a while. Didn't do anything for the rubbery taste in her mouth, though.

The growls, howls, and barks from the bedroom weren't helping her growing headache. Janie, her two-year-old pit bull girl, was *not* happy about all this brouhaha, and wanted the whole neighborhood to know it.

Finally the last box was set down, the last papers signed. With more relief than the situation probably warranted, Trisha let out her breath in a loud whoosh, shut the door to #3, and let Janie out of the bedroom before collapsing in a chair at the sparkly chrome and red Formica dinette.

Janie *whuffed* at her, and began sniffing her way around the tiny kitchen, then the living room. She paid special attention to anything the three strange humans had touched, hackles rising and falling as the investigation proceeded around and through the assorted boxes of her life.

Trisha hoped Janie wouldn't mess the floor in her excitement, but at least pee wouldn't show on the horrid yellow vinyl.

Oh well. The place was cheap, clean, and most importantly, close to public transit. She wasn't quite ready to tackle driving with her new leg, but physical therapy was going well. Maybe by Christmas she'd rent a car and give it a shot.

Finally satisfied, Janie wrapped up her inspection. She trotted back to Trisha, showing all her teeth in a vicious smile before sitting at her feet and plonking her blocky brindled head on Trisha's knee.

"So whatcha think, girlie girl? This place meet your approval?"

She scratched Janie's ears, earning a groan as her undocked pibble tail went to work sweeping the floor.

Trisha groaned herself when someone knocked on the door. Didn't she deserve at least a few minutes off her feet, both flesh and plastic?

She pushed her way up from the chair and limped to the door. Checking through the peephole, she saw an unruly mop of curly copper hair over a pale, tired face. A male face. One that needed a shave.

She made sure the safety chain was in place, and cracked the door.

"Hi," the guy said. "I'm Bill Jackson. Your neighbor in #2. Welcome to the building."

Trisha looked him up and down as Janie did her ferocious guard dog thing, hiding behind Trisha's legs and whining. She reached down to scratch the big coward's ears.

Bill looked to be in his early thirties, around her age. Not chubby, not thin. But not much muscle tone, and eerily pale. More pale than the red hair warranted, surely. But not sickly. Black t-shirt and blue jeans. Birkenstock sandals on his feet. He was holding a paper sack stained with grease marks, and a steaming carafe which smelled like heaven. Coffee, and something beyond the Mr. variety.

"What do you think, Janie? Do we open the door?"

Janie *whuffed*, but stayed behind her. *This guy is new*, that whuff said, *but doesn't seem too dangerous*.

"I promise I'm harmless," the guy confirmed, backing away a step and lifting the pitcher and the sack. "I bring offerings of fresh-roasted coffee and almost fresh apple fritters."

The fritters did it. Her stomach grumbled as she shut the door, slid the chain, and opened up again.

"Come on in. My name's Trisha Macintyre, and this is Janie. She promises not to eat you, if you behave."

She thought his face went even paler, but he stepped in and she shut the screen door behind him, leaving the main door open.

Maybe a cross breeze would help air the place out.

CHAPTER 3

*B*ill looked around the apartment as he followed his new neighbor inside. Not that he needed a distraction from her pert derriere, not at all. Her slight limp caused everything to rock in a fascinating way.

Damn she was pretty.

And not that he was scared of the giant brown and black-streaked behemoth in front of her. Not at all.

Trisha was an inch or so shorter than his own five-eleven. Okay, five-ten and a half. Honey-colored hair fell in a thick curtain to her shoulders, and she had that golden tan and hazel eyes that seemed exclusive to blonde women in the southwest.

Her broad shoulders tapered down to a narrow waist. Long legs all the way to the floor, nicely accentuated in blue jeans. Her left foot was bare, but she had a heavy black sneaker on her right. Weird.

Then he saw the elbow crutches leaning against the door. The limp must be something more serious than a sprain.

None of his business, of course.

She fetched a couple of mugs from a box and set them on the table. Bill sat down and poured the coffee while Trisha ripped a couple of paper towels from a roll on the counter.

Bill tried to ignore the dog as it paced around the floor. Was it eyeballing *him*, or the pastries?

Trisha finally quit puttering and flopped into the chair across from his. Her dog laid down beside her. Bill handed her a fritter and took a big bite of his own.

"Thank you so much," she said. "I haven't even started unpacking, and the day's been so busy I never got around to ordering takeout."

She bit into the fritter. "Oh my god," she said, her eyes widening and then closing in bliss. "This is absolutely amazing!"

"Glad you like it. There's a place just down the road that makes them fresh every morning. I usually grab a couple on the way home from work."

"On the way home? Are you a nightbird?" She took a drink of coffee. Licked her lips with a perfect pink tongue.

Down boy.

"Yeah, I work graveyard at a data center. We do all the maintenance and batch jobs at night, when load is low."

"Oh no," she said, flushing as she opened her eyes and stared at him in dismay. "I bet we woke you up with all the delivery noise. I'm so sorry!"

"Forget it," he said, looking away from her eyes and lips. "I needed to get up anyway."

They nibbled fritters and drank coffee. Bill never knew what to say to people, and was just fine waiting for her to speak. Finally, she did.

"So is that your green Caddy down in the garage? The '59 de Ville? Those fins would suit a whale."

"That would be *my* car, Ms. Macintyre," said a voice through the screen door. Bill looked out and saw a short, barrel-chested *Chicano* in faded dungarees and red checked shirt. Graying hair topped a cheerful face with deep smile creases at the corners of his nut-brown eyes. "*El corcel del emperador. The Emperor's mighty steed.*"

"Hey, Manny," Bill said, raising his hand. To Trisha, he said, "You've met Manuel Ortega, right? The owner?"

"Oh yes," she said, smiling. "Come on in, Mr. Ortega! Bill here was kind enough to bring me aid and succor, in the form of donuts and coffee."

"No, no. These are not donuts, young lady.

These are apple fritters, and worthy of the great gods of old Mexico. And you must call me Manny."

"Don't let Manny fool you, Trisha. He's American as apple pie."

Trisha's pit bull raised its head, popped to its feet, and went for Manny, baring its vicious teeth.

"Watch out, Manny! The dog—"

He stopped when Manny reached down to ruffle the dog's ears with his thick hands.

"Si, eres una buena chica, ¿no?"

The beast's whole back half wagged. The thumping of its tail against its ribs sounded like a bass drum.

"Big, strong man like you, afraid of this pretty girl. Tsk."

Bill didn't ask which pretty girl Manny referred to.

"But it was snarling," Bill said, looking at Trisha. "That was a snarl, right?"

"That was a smile," Trisha said, her own mouth quirking at the corners. "Janie always smiles at people she likes, dontcha Snarla Jane?"

Janie snarled her way back to Trisha on stiff legs, tail now going in circles like a propeller.

"Buena chica," Manny said again, grinning at the dog. "Forgive him, Ms. Macintyre. He was attacked by a vicious canine as a boy, and still has nightmares."

"What happened?" Trisha asked, hands going to her mouth.

"I was six. I was cutting through a neighbor's backyard," Bill said, feeling heat in his cheeks. "Their dog saw me and came after me. I got over the fence, but not before it took a chunk out of my butt. Nastiest schnauzer you ever saw."

"Well, Snarla Jane won't bite you, I promise. At least as long as you don't bang anything. She hates sudden loud noises. But you don't have to snuggle her at night, either."

They all laughed, even if Bill had to force it a little.

"Bill, would you maybe have time to help me unload a couple rolls of flooring before you go to work?" Manny said. "They're in the truck around back."

"Sure," Bill said, getting up and dusting stray bits of sugar from his shirt. "Trisha, it's very nice to meet you. See you around."

"Bye, Bill. Thanks for the food and the coffee. Drop by in the morning and I'll whip you up some dinner to repay you." She smiled and patted his hand, but didn't get up.

Bill and Manny left the apartment and made their way down the central stair to the loading area behind the building.

"So what you think of her, eh?" Manny said,

waggling his eyebrows. *"Muy bonita,* don't you think?"

"I'm not big on dogs, but she seems house-broken and friendly enough."

Manny punched his shoulder.

"Don't play the smart kid with me, Bill. You know what I mean."

"Yeah, I reckon she's pretty enough. What's up with the crutches? She on the mend from something?"

"You could say, yeah. She was in a wreck last year. Some drunk ran a red light and t-boned the car she and her fiancé were in. Crushed the passenger door. They got her out, but her leg…well, she lost it below the knee. Just now getting to where she's okay on her own. She took this place to get out of her mama's house. I think they get along okay, but she needs to be on her own, you know?"

Wow. Okay. That explained the limp and the big black shoe.

"What happened to her fiancé? They postpone the wedding?"

"Oh yeah. They postponed it all right." Manny spat on the pavement. "The dirty *pendejo* decided she wasn't whole anymore and kicked her to the curb."

"Man, that sucks. I hate that for her."

"So show it," Manny said as they reached a

pickup loaded down with a lot more than a couple of rolls of vinyl floor. "Ask her to dinner. Walk her dog if she needs it. Flowers. Wine. Candy. All that shit."

"Flowers and candy I can do. But she has to walk her own dog."

"Bill, Bill, Bill. I thought you had a brain in that fuzzy pale head of yours."

CHAPTER 4

$\mathcal{T}$risha was enjoying having her own place again.

Over the next three weeks, she and Janie settled into their routine. Not much of one, really. Trisha was living on the insurance money from the accident, which should last her another couple of years if she stayed smart and didn't waste it.

No, she and Janie stayed close to home. Manny sometimes took her grocery shopping in his gas-guzzling road whale. Sometimes Bill invited her over for a meal. Breakfast for him, dinner for her. He even set down a dish for Janie, though Trisha could tell her horrible, evil, vicious pibble made him nervous.

He *should* be nervous. Janie could lick the skin from a t-rex when she really got going. Best exfoliation on the planet.

She smiled as she puttered through the kitchen. This morning she'd make dinner for him, breakfast for her. A good vegetable frittata and some crusty rye bread. She'd started everything when he'd gotten off the bus fifteen minutes ago.

The eggs had about ten more minutes to go. Plenty of time to take Janie out for a quick trot through the grass, since Bill was probably still in the shower.

"Go easy on mommy, girlie girl," Trisha said as she eased down the stairs. Her thigh muscles were getting stronger every day, but she still had to watch her balance on stairs and ramps.

Janie stayed by her side, the leash limp as they went.

On the traffic-filled boulevard, four lanes of cars and trucks zoomed in either direction, inches from the sidewalk.

Just before the bottom step, the worst thing happened.

Trisha's right foot was on the way down when a faded delivery van backfired, belching sparks and black smoke like an old-fashioned cannon.

Janie gave a high-pitched *yike* and lunged, pulling her leash out of Trisha's grip.

Trisha lost her balance, coming down on her fake foot at the wrong angle.

She screamed as she heard the artificial ankle snap.

As she watched her baby streak across the sidewalk and into the street.

All Trisha could do was hit the ground and begin crawling after her.

"JANIE!!" someone yelled. The same someone jumped over Trisha and pelted toward the now honking and braking vehicles.

She saw pale skin, red hair, and boxers covered with the Batman signal.

Bill ran barefoot right into the traffic, hands held out toward the oncoming cars.

Sweet Jesus, Janie was on the median. Darting back and forth, barking her fool head off.

CHAPTER 5

Bill ignored the pain in his bare feet as he shot out into the traffic.

On the concrete divider, Trisha's dog…Janie… ran back and forth. He finally got to her and grabbed her leash. She reared up and punched him in the thighs with both front feet.

Try to help and get bruises for your trouble.

Bill wound the leash around and around his hand, choking up until no slack remained.

How the hell was he going to get her back across the road?

This was Vegas after all, and people on the way to or from their busy lives weren't going to slow down for something as mundane as a dog and a mostly naked computer guy in the road.

"Okay, Janie. Here's what's going to happen.

I'm going to pick you up, and you are *not* going to bite or struggle. Sound good to you?"

Jesus, he was talking to a dumb dog.

Still gripping the leash, he knelt down and gathered Janie in his arms. Wow. She had to weigh eighty pounds.

Tremors ran through her stiff body, but she held still. And kept quiet, except for a tiny little whine that tugged at his heartstrings.

"Gonna be okay, girl. Just close your eyes and—"

He broke off as a green-finned missile shot from the garage beneath the apartment building, barreling straight across the sidewalk and across both southbound lanes.

Tires squealed and brakes smoked. Horns blared and fists waved. Cars swerved and skewed.

But somehow didn't hit each other.

Manny jumped out of the Caddy, popping a couple of flares which he waved at the now-still vehicles like a maniacal gunslinger.

"*Andale*, Bill! Get your ass in gear!" he bellowed.

Bill didn't need telling twice.

Still holding the (incredibly heavy) Janie, he ran back across the road toward where Trisha held out her arms.

"I got...I got Jan...Janie..." he panted, setting

both the pibble and his own self down. He put the leash in Trisha's hand.

She threw her arms around Janie and kissed all over her blocky head. Janie returned it all with her raspy tongue.

Bill tried not to have a heart attack as he gulped in the dry desert air.

Manny pulled his road boat back across and into the garage. He killed the engine and strolled casually over to Bill and Trisha.

"Not bad," he said. "Not bad at all. Not for a *gringo*."

"Say thank you to the nice man, Janie," Trisha said, wiping tears and slobber away with the palm of her hand. She grinned at Bill through her tears, and his heart skipped a little.

Damn, she was pretty.

Janie showed Bill all her gleaming teeth, then proceeded to lick his face raw.

And wonder of wonders, he wasn't scared a bit. Not even when Trisha pushed Janie out of the way to add her own kiss.

CHAPTER 6

"So how's the new foot?" Manny asked as Bill held the Caddy's rear door for Trisha. He'd been kind enough to drive them to the squat gray prosthetics center for Trisha's final fitting on her replacement leg.

The bells of a nearby church rang six times. Trisha glanced at her watch, startled at how late it was. The fitting, testing, adjusting, and all the other stuff that went along with second-hand feet had gone on longer than she'd realized. But Bill had been there the whole way, chatting with her and the white-clad doctor/mechanic. She hadn't noticed the time at all.

"Good as new," Trisha said, grinning. She loved how they'd been able to match her skin tone almost perfectly. She might even break out a pair of shorts.

"Better, even. It's a whole new spring design, so it should last through any unplanned trips."

The knee socket also fit far more comfortably. She felt like walking all the way home, or maybe dancing all the way.

Bill chuckled as he got in beside her. She still wasn't completely sure about this whole dating-her-neighbor thing, but so far so good. Janie approved, always wagging her way to Bill and licking his hands. Bill was also more at ease by the day, tolerating Janie's affections and even rubbing her ears when he thought no one was watching. The two must've bonded out there on that median.

Janie's approval went a long way toward easing Trisha's mind.

"Where to now?" Manny said as he reached over to the passenger seat to rub Janie's ears. *"Buena chica* says we should go get some apple fritters."

Manny had offered to take Janie for a walk in the park while they waited on Bill and Trisha, but she smelled something suspiciously like cheeseburger on her baby's breath.

"I'm sure she does," Trisha said. "But between you and Bill, Janie's starting to get a bit of a belly on her. How about you take us home, and we can order some pizza?"

"Yes, madame. Home it is. But I will leave you

three to your pizza, as I am an old man and need to hit the bed soon."

"That's a damn shame, Manny," Bill said. "I guess it'll just be me and Snarla Jane helping Trisha with the pizza."

He squeezed her hand and smiled at her. She smiled back, amazed at how something as simple as a truck's backfire could change her life so much.

In the front seat, Janie *whuffed* as her tail thumped against the seat as Trisha leaned over to kiss Bill's sweet face.

The Heart
IS THE
STRONGEST

KARI KILGORE

AUTHOR OF MORNING GLORY AND THE SWEETEST TROUBLE

For Jason

Who understands peculiar magic

CHAPTER 1

*M*ost of the time, Craig Douglas was nothing but glad he'd moved back home.

Lightning Gap, Virginia, was a welcome change of pace after seventeen years in Atlanta. Hidden away high up in the Blue Ridge Mountains, with one end of the main road through town passing by a stunning overlook of row after row of mountains way off into the distance.

Craig had always thought they looked like gigantic blue-green ocean waves during summer, and what he imagined the ocean would look like if it instantly froze solid in the winter.

This time of year, late into October with November knocking on the door, the waves transformed again, shifting toward a resting cold-weather gray. A few streaks and spots of green remained from pines and cedars, but the blazing finery of red, orange, and yellow from a few weeks back was almost gone.

The sharp, crisp air was a welcome change against his skin, especially compared to what could still be muggy and warm back in Atlanta. Here at four thousand feet above sea level, highs hovered in the fifties before dropping to around freezing at night. The incredibly blue sky didn't carry a trace of Atlanta's haze, as if everything in Craig's sight (and a lot of things in his heart and mind) had been washed clean by the fierce thunderstorms that gave Lightning Gap its name.

His parents' house was tucked into the forest just outside of the tiny alpine tourist town, a sturdy wood-frame Craftsman bungalow with a deep screened-in sitting porch. His father's pride and joy, the still-green lawn, and his mother's prize-winning flower gardens framed the house and marked it as a well-loved retirement home.

Drifting traces of someone's wood stove smoke scented the air, cutting through the earthy aroma of the fallen leaves turning themselves into compost. Even well into his forties and a long way past family camping trips, those smells together always set up a craving for hot dogs and campfire s'mores in Craig's belly.

Being able to get in his car and drive or even walk

the more direct but steep trail down into Lightning Gap in a few minutes, no matter the time of day or night, might have turned into his favorite thing about the house. Even if they needed to go on into Bountyfield or Hidden Springs for shopping or one of his parents' doctor visits, he knew exactly how long it would take.

No mystery traffic jams, with vehicles at a standstill for an solid hour for no apparent reason. No sitting in an endless line of cars creeping along at two miles an hour every morning and every night. No marinating in the stinking exhaust of a thousand other cars in oppressive heat, seeping through the tightest window seals and defeating the icebox of air conditioning.

Nope, back here the drive was reliably a mile a minute once you got past the twisty roads and out of town. Trips took the same amount of time, every time.

Until they didn't.

Once in a great while, as in once in the eight months since Craig arrived, a wreck or a fallen tree would jam things up. The huge problem then was there was no other way *to* go. Unless you happened to be sitting right beside a questionable back road, you were sitting. And still, somehow that wasn't nearly as annoying as fuming and stewing in constant city traffic.

Right at that moment, though, Craig had the

hardest wish he'd had yet to be back in the middle of snarling, seething, steel and concrete madness.

During a spectacular thunderstorm the night before, a gigantic oak had crashed across the end of the curving gravel driveway. A tree Craig had loved since the first time he saw this house when his parents retired and moved up here from Wolf Branch. It had always kept him connected somehow, grounded. Now instead of towering and comforting him, the trunk had to be eighty feet long and almost as tall as Craig at just over six feet.

If that had been all, he might have (unwisely) convinced himself that of course he could clear the giant out himself. Just go into the garage, grab the chainsaw he hadn't touched since he was an early teenager, and get to work.

Of course the background worry of needing an ambulance for one of his parents would have turned into glaring reality of having to call one for himself, and in record speed.

Thank goodness his father had vetoed that idea first thing that morning, before coffee and before Craig's pride had forced him to offer. After making his unsteady way out to the porch with Craig's mother fluttering and fussing in circles around him, the elder Mr. Douglas had declared the tree way too big for anyone without a crane truck and professional chainsaws to handle.

Craig hadn't pretended to argue, but he had at

least put on old blue jeans, a faded t-shirt, and a respectable denim jacket for the occasion. Just in case he could actually contribute in some way.

So now he waited, alternating between fuming at having his way blocked—even if he actually didn't *need* to go anywhere right now—and relieved someone in Lightning Gap had the equipment to rescue them all. The short couple of miles between him and town felt like total isolation at the moment

He paced back and forth on that broad porch with more coffee, fighting the urge to check his watch, and refusing to go back inside and get his parents as agitated as he was.

"Calm down, city boy," he said under his breath. "You came back here to leave all that rush and hurry and stress bullshit behind, remember?"

But he still heaved a huge sigh of relief and rolled his eyes when he heard the distinct grind of a big truck shifting gears on the steep road below the house. That was almost certainly a big truck of the tree-removing variety, and some poor unlucky driver doing his level best to figure out how to navigate the vicious switchback down below the house.

Their rescuers had arrived.

CHAPTER 2

Sophie Edwards groaned when she got a good look at the sharp curve in the blacktop road ahead, which she would have sworn turned more than 180 degrees as it headed up the heavily forested mountain. In the back of her mind, she knew that was only an illusion because the blasted roadbed climbed a good twenty feet in that curve.

But she would still like to have a long, possibly loud conversation with whoever thought cutting a road through here was any kind of sensible idea.

Clearly someone who'd never driven a massive diesel truck hauling a tree crane on a trailer with a load of tools along behind it. A truck with a lovely permanent smell of fresh-cut wood, overly bouncy front seats, and the tendency to stall out at low speeds even in low gear if you didn't know just how to coax it along.

She glanced over at her big brother George, currently doing his "stare straight ahead and don't say a word" routine. Sophie appreciated that most of the time far more than his annoying older sibling routine of telling her how she was doing everything wrong. She'd learned how to drive this persnickety crane truck the same way he had: at their father's affectionate insistence.

And most of the time, she was thankful to her dad and her brother for refusing to coddle her when she decided to get out of fifteen years of graphic and website design and into this crazy tree clearing business a year ago. Back when a couple of other changes in her life turned her boring but tolerable career into a cage she was desperate to get out of in a few quick months.

Moving from Hidden Springs back up to Lightning Gap, working outdoors, and tackling new challenges she chose for herself and could actually conquer had been exactly what she needed.

Her father and her brother both let her take on anything she wanted to learn, from running the crane to swinging an axe to getting the chain back on a chainsaw. So far, she loved pretty much everything about the job.

At the moment, though, facing a monster

switchback, she wouldn't have minded a bit of George's endless coaching.

She dropped the truck's transmission down again, riding the clutch to keep the silly thing from stalling itself out in the curve. Then she hauled the big steering wheel around and hit the gas at just the right moment. Sophie grinned as the trailer swung itself into line without even scraping into the gravel at the side of the road.

She couldn't resist sneaking another glance at George as she straightened the truck back out and headed on up the mountain. He kept up the staring game for a few more seconds before he nodded and flashed her a half-smile.

"Good driving, kid. That one would have challenged the old man. Not that he would have admitted it."

"Kid?" Sophie said, shaking her head. "I'm forty-three, Georgie. How old do I have to get before you cut that one out?"

"Not until you catch up with me, I'm afraid." He pointed ahead and to the left, where a gravel driveway cut away from the blacktop. "I think that's our victim's house. I've never been out this way. Sound like they're going to be trouble?"

Sophie slowed again, getting ready for a much more gentle curve.

"I only talked to one of them, sounded like he was our age. A bit high-strung, or at least nervous and trying not to show it. Taking care of his parents, both in bad health, and did I *understand* that this was urgent, all that."

She didn't mention what a dead sexy voice the guy had, how she could have listened to him all day, even in his obvious "I'm doing my best to be calm but please hurry" state.

Just then she got a good look at the damage and whistled.

"Well, he was being honest about the mess. This one's gonna take a while."

The oak sprawled across the lawn and driveway was easily over a hundred years old, probably one of the first to grow back up after the whole area was clear-cut down to muddy nothing in the days of the old timber barons. The branches that hadn't broken off stood nearly as tall as the neat bungalow house itself.

Sophie felt the same melancholy pang she always did when a tree that old had breathed its last. Renewable resources and all that, and a long life well-lived. Much as she enjoyed the work and no matter how many times she saw this, that touch of sadness still worked its way in.

"Lucky that one didn't hit the house," George said, pulling a worn and faded blue baseball cap over his curly black hair. "And too bad all that wood's too green for the big bonfire in town tomorrow night."

"I think this beauty might give us bonfire wood for a few years."

She got the truck parked and the brake solidly set, then pulled her own unruly hair back into a ponytail. One thing she hadn't quite managed to accept about this new job was the Edwards family uniform of gray canvas coveralls. Sure, they were durable and easy to wash, and kept the clothes underneath relatively clean. But Sophie was still vain enough, or maybe simply aware enough to realize she'd never found a pair that didn't make her look shapeless and dreadful.

Washing, mending, and keeping up her supply of sturdy jeans, cotton shirts, and whichever flannel shirt she grabbed on the way out the door was worth it to keep her from feeling like she'd disappeared completely.

By the time she and George made it across the lawn to survey the damage, a guy dressed head to toe in denim walked toward them on the other side of the huge trunk. He had wavy brown hair starting to get a bit shaggy around the edges, and a reddish goatee that he'd either stopped shaving or decided to let grow into a beard.

Once she got got close enough to see the tension in and around eyes as blue as the October sky, Sophie decided he had to be the one she'd talked to on the phone. She hadn't expected him to be nearly as cute as his voice sounded through his worry.

"Thank you for getting here so fast," he said, reaching up over the deep grooves of the trunk to shake their hands with a warm, firm grip. "Craig Douglas. I'm amazed you made it around that curve on the first try."

George waved his hand at Sophie.

"That was all my kid sister's great driving. Sophie's a natural with that beast of a truck."

Craig's eyes widened and he smiled, but not in that leering way Sophie had grown to dislike intensely enough to daydream about using their biggest axe as a deterrent. He looked impressed, and attentive in a way that made her wish her big brother wasn't going to be here all day, too.

And thank the gods she'd decided to pass on the coveralls.

"Well," Craig said, shaking his head, "it took me a while to figure out how to navigate that road in a sedan when my parents moved up here twenty years ago. You definitely have my respect. I'll help as much as I can if that's okay. I always loved that old tree. I wouldn't mind sending it on its way, maybe keeping a bit of the wood. Otherwise I'll be happy to bring out coffee or water or whatever you want. My mother may not always remember to scold me these days, but she made sure I'd never forget my manners."

Sophie felt a slow smile curving her lips, and little flutter of excitement in her belly that she thought she'd banished forever after leaving Sinking Springs. And leaving Zach.

"We sure do appreciate the offer," she said. "Of help and coffee, especially as good as yours smells. Insurance won't let you get too close with the crane or the big saws going, but you can help load up the branches when the time comes."

CHAPTER 3

After a long day of running out water and coffee, helping his mother bring some of her outrageously good peanut cinnamon oatmeal cookies she still remembered how to bake (funny how that part lingered), and helping load up what seemed like a thousand oak branches, Craig was so weary and sore he could hardly move.

And entirely enchanted with Sophie.

He could admit to a somewhat stereotypical reaction to how strong she was, how secure and comfortable she looked working with her brother. Whether she used the biggest chainsaw he'd ever seen to break down the massive tree trunk, operated the crane to swing logs easily ten feet long onto the trailer, or gathered up a massive armful of branches, his gaze was constantly drawn back to her.

But that wasn't what had him honestly dreading the end of the exhausting day.

The air fairly crackled around Sophie, from her gorgeous green eyes to her shining black hair. Mostly from her words and her expressions, though, the sharp intelligence that she never bothered trying to hide.

Craig had caught that with other people throughout his life, that spark that captured his attention for as long as they both could stand it. A few guys, a few women. A handful of months or even a few years of a relationship so intense it couldn't help but burn itself out.

One of the many reasons he'd left Atlanta was to give himself a break. Reset his circuitry, maybe, figure out a way to be with a partner without getting so consumed. Giving all of that intensity and drama up now that he was getting older made all kinds of sense.

Until he met Sophie.

And realized how much he'd missed that connection.

How much he honestly needed it.

He'd gotten so far into his own head—and into trying to stretch his aching back without anyone noticing—that Sophie had to touch his shoulder to get his attention.

The sparks flared up into a flame.

"Sorry, off gathering wool," he said. "Or gathering branches, I should say."

She laughed and nodded. "Yeah, this job can drain you head to toe. You said you wanted to keep some of the wood? Were you thinking branches, or maybe something big enough for furniture? We can haul it all off, but I figure the tree lived all those years in your family's yard, so the whole thing is yours if you want it."

Craig stared at the massive pile, trying to imagine what all of that lumber could turn into. A whole house as far as he could tell. But he probably needed to think a good bit smaller.

"I hadn't thought about furniture. Do you know someone who knows how to do that? Someone close by?"

"I sure do." She glanced at her brother, who was trying to hid his smile for some reason. "We both do. A couple of our cousins do everything from tables and chairs to cabinets to sculptures. They often buy the bigger pieces from us or the homeowners."

Craig had to admit the idea of being in touch with someone Sophie knew sounded like a good plan. Maybe a good excuse to stay in touch with her.

"Are they local?"

"They're down in Bountyfield, over in Boun County. But they'll be here tomorrow for the big festival here in Lightning Gap. They'll have a lot of their stuff available, so you can look at it and get some ideas, maybe."

This time her brother snorted, turned bright red, and walked across the trampled but cleared lawn toward the truck.

Sophie rolled her eyes and scowled at his back.

"Okay, what my dear brother George is trying not to say, or trying to get *me* to say, is I'd be glad to introduce you to our cousins. Want to go to the festival with me?"

That was the other thing about when Craig met someone who had that energy that matched so well with his. Almost without fail, they *both* felt it.

"You know, I've never been," he said. "My parents both loved it years back, but I never happened to be up here at the right time. I'd love to, Sophie."

She nodded once and smiled.

"Good. Since you can get out of your driveway now, want to meet me down there tomorrow afternoon? Say around six? You don't want to miss the big bonfire, but that way you won't have to be there too long."

"I don't think that will be too long," Craig said. "I'd say I'd just walk but I may not be able to go even two miles after today. Let me make sure I can get someone in to help with my parents, but six sounds good to me."

After Sophie and her brother left, with her driving the big truck again, Craig wandered across the battered grass, trying to stretch his legs and back and gathering up a few big handfuls of the giant's last crop of acorns. He wasn't quite sure why.

But they felt as good in his hands and pockets as the idea of spending more time with Sophie did to his heart and mind.

CHAPTER 4

At 5:30 the next afternoon, Sophie leaned against one of the sturdy wooden railings around the wide open area along the outskirts of Lighting Gap that everyone called the fairgrounds. Not because there were permanent exhibit spaces or barns, or even because they actually held any kind of fair there most years.

It was just one of those habits in a small town. No one knew when it started or why. But no one felt particularly inclined to change it.

Past the broad grass and gravel space behind her, the ridgeline rose up sharp and spectacular. The nearly vertical layers of limestone that broke through the hardwoods and pines gave witness to the violent birth of the mountains all around. Sophie had often tried to imagine what the truly gigantic mountain that stood here looked like before it washed away, finding its way down the Mississippi eons ago to help build Louisiana.

The fairgrounds was jammed full of a feast for the senses, and a bit of overload on all counts. No carnival rides tonight, but a surprisingly good bluegrass band competed with giggly, shrieking children and the saws her cousins brought to demonstrate their work. Fresh popcorn warred with roasting chicken and the lovely scent of fresh cut wood.

A bunch of local artists were set up in rows, with colorful displays of quilts, paintings, and every kind of sculpture under the sun. Odds and Endings Bookstore had a huge section full of books, along with local and visiting authors who'd spent time there.

What might look like a makeshift haunted house made up of various tents set up together managed to keep herds of kids and more than a few adults scared and entertained in equal measure.

Sophie had arrived far too early partly out of excitement about seeing Craig again, but also out of a nervous inability to focus on anything else all day long. She'd spent a ridiculous amount of time rooting through her closet, trying on clothes she hadn't even looked at since she moved back home. In the end, she'd settled on clean blue jeans and a green sweater she knew set off her eyes nicely.

She had a jacket in her car in case the clear night chill got to be too much, but she doubted that would be a problem. She was way too anxious to get cold.

Despite asking a man she'd only met the day before out on a date, that wasn't the reason for her agitation. She had the odd feeling something else was going on. Something coming that she couldn't quite see or figure out. She'd gotten that sense a few times in her life, but she could usually get an idea what got her so stirred up.

When she spotted Craig walking across the graveled parking lot toward her, she wondered if it wasn't him she was reacting to after all.

He'd transformed himself from cute and tense and fascinating into more of a *wow, where did you* come *from?* status. Black jeans and a deep burgundy shirt intensified his eyes, and his smile when he saw Sophie made her weak in the knees.

Even her mind's whispers that she didn't want to get into all the stuff and nonsense of a relationship again dropped down to a low, resentful mutter.

"You look wonderful, Sophie," he said, leaning against the rail beside her.

"You're easy on the eyes yourself, Craig. Get everything settled with your parents okay?"

He nodded, but his smile turned sad. "Yeah, they're okay. Mom's been a bit agitated since that big tree fell, but she likes the woman who comes to sit with them when I'm out. Dad did fine coping with her memory trouble until he broke his leg last year. Now he… She gets around perfectly fine, but he doesn't. They just need a bit more help."

Sophie nodded, resisting the urge to put her arm around him.

"My dad's been fighting having to slow down like a wildcat. He still gets out on a lot of jobs, but he's turning more and more over to me and Georgie."

"Good thing we're both here for them, huh?" Craig actually winked, and Sophie burst into laughter.

She was convinced he knew she'd come back home to give *herself* a break, and being able to help someone else had been just a bonus.

She had the strongest feeling that was true for him, too.

"Your parents are real sweethearts," she said. "They're lucky to have you. Now that we're here, let me show you around the place. I've got a surprise for you, too."

When Craig surprised her by holding out his arm, she surprised herself by taking it as they walked out into the harvest festival.

CHAPTER 5

Craig wasn't sure how such a small space—
barely the size of a couple of the football
fields that were so all-important to the local social
scene—could seem so vast and exciting and vibrant.
He felt as if he'd walked out into the middle of the
vast acreage of the Midtown Arts Festival in
Atlanta, but with bluegrass rather than whatever
music was trendy that year.

The crackling sharp evening air was surely part
of it. But not nearly as much as having Sophie
pressed warm and close against him. With her
amazing curls loose and free in the breeze, whatever
sparkled around her turned itself up to eleven.
Something inside him, held tense and tight for
longer than he could remember, relaxed and luxuri-
ated in her company.

He tried not to kick himself too hard over

blurting out so much about his parents when he'd barely said hello. Apparently Sophie had dealt with a little bit of the same, but still.

Great way to make a bad first impression.

At least the conversation between them stayed lighter now, more free, as they strolled along and admired the remarkable skills of artists from in and around Lightning Gap. The crowded area where Sophie's cousins worked wasn't far ahead, the buzz of a chainsaw and sharp bite of freshly cut wood leading the way. He'd been looking forward to the possibilities for the old oak tree almost as much as walking arm in arm with Sophie.

Craig almost didn't look at his phone when it started buzzing in his pocket.

He answered with a shaking hand when he saw the number.

"Mrs. Holbrook? Anything wrong?"

She only sobbed in his ear for a second, and he reluctantly stepped away from Sophie. Mrs. Holbrook spoke so fast he could barely catch the words.

"Oh honey, I'm so sorry. I only turned my back for a second, just to help your dad."

"It's okay. Slow down and tell me what's going on."

Sophie frowned and reached for Craig's hand, and he was happy to grab hold.

"I'm *so* sorry! Your dad was trying to get a book

off the shelf and he dropped it, so I helped him get it and get settled. When I turned around, you know how *fast* your mom is."

Craig's throat tightened up and he closed his eyes. The noise and light and smells all around him clashed and roared in his mind.

"Is she okay?" he said through his teeth.

"I don't *know*! The front door was standing open, and by the time I got out to the porch I couldn't see her. I called and called and your dad did too, but she was gone."

Craig took a deep breath and looked into Sophie's wide green eyes. As much as he didn't want to see him trying to struggle through this latest crisis, a scared-half-to-death part of him was glad she was there.

"Okay," he said. "Okay. Did you call the sheriff's department?"

"Of course I did, honey, right before I called you. They're out looking for her right now."

"Good. Is Dad all right?"

Craig heard muttering on the other end, then Mrs. Holbrook came back on.

"He's upset, like we all are. I asked if he wanted to talk to you, but keeps saying find her, find her. What do you want me to do, Craig? I can load him up in the car and help search."

"No, I think it's better if you stay there if you can." Craig kept his visions of Mrs. Holbrook, upset herself and trying to keep his father calm, not seeing his mother step out into the road in front of the car. "She's never tried to go off like this before. Has she when I've been gone?"

"Not at all. She keeps herself too busy trying to take care of your dad."

"She does. I'm going to see what I can find out. I'll call you if I hear anything, and you do the same."

He shook his head, staring up at the cold, bright stars staring to come out overhead.

Of all the nights for his mother's behavior to take such a sudden change.

Of all the nights for him to be here instead of at home.

Sophie squeezed his hand.

"What can I do?"

CHAPTER 6

Sophie's heart clenched tight in her chest at the frightened look in Craig's eyes.

"I don't... I have no idea. The sheriffs are already out looking for her. Are there speakers here? Some kind of announcement system?"

"Nothing like that, but I can get us the next best thing. My cousins will have every kid in town who's not at the haunted house gathered around."

She was glad and more than a little touched that he held on to her hand and let her lead the way.

Sophie didn't want to think about Craig's sweet mother walking along the road, much less wandering off in the steep woods around their house. She'd lost her own mother much too young to really remember her. So she'd always felt a curious mix of envy and happiness for anyone who had both parents long enough to see them get old.

Even when terrifying problems like dementia were part of the package.

She caught sight of her cousin Rick and his husband Michael through the crowd, both of them wearing what they called their Standard Issue Butch Lumberjack outfits of black and red checked flannel. Her cousin Mary stood close by, using a fine chisel only a few inches long on the carving in front of her. Even from a few yards away, Sophie expected the life-sized dog in rich yellow and brown tones to come to life, wag her tail, and bound off through the piles of sawdust on the ground.

Just like Sophie expected, a bunch of early teenagers were gathered around Rick and Michael and their small but noisy chainsaws.

"They'll round up the kids in a flash," she said, turning to Craig. "Do you have a picture of…"

He'd stopped walking, staring into the crowd ahead. At a wisp of fluffy silver hair moving around back, where stacks of wood waited.

"Mom?" Craig said under his breath, stepping forward and pulling Sophie along with him.

The hair moved forward, and Sophie recognized Craig's mother. She seemed perfectly calm and serene, her blue pants matching her jacket, with not a hair or a button out of place.

Sophie waved to get Rick's attention, then pointed toward the stacks of wood.

Craig sagged against her when he saw his

mother reach out for one of the big square pieces, bright yellow and heavy.

"That *is* her. How the hell did she get all the way down here?"

He leaned over and kissed Sophie's cheek before he circled around to his mother's side.

By the time Sophie caught up, still smiling in combined relief and from the tingles his lips sent shooting through her, he had his arm around his mother. Rick caught Sophie's eye, then headed back out front when she nodded.

"What are you doing out here, Mom?" Craig said. "Dad and Mrs. Holbrook are worried sick."

His mother pursed her lips and scowled at him, a sign of dismissal so clear Sophie had to choke back a laugh. Her remarkably smooth skin looked even younger under the soft lighting.

"I had to get the heart before they took all of our tree away," she said, resting her hand on the rough block of wood. "The heart of the whole tree. Our house won't be right without it, you know. Your father doesn't always understand about these things. But you do, don't you?"

"I do, Mom. I sure do." Craig looked at Sophie, tears standing in his eyes. "Is this…"

"Your tree," Sophie said. "Sure is. That was the surprise I told you about earlier. All the rest is in storage so it can dry out. Mary makes these gorgeous carvings that last for years and years, but they're meant to weather and crack and warp and get more beautiful over time. She says they're a lot like people that way. I asked her if she'd make one for you tonight."

Craig sighed and smiled, then reached his free hand out to Sophie.

"Is this the heartwood?" he said. "Is that what Mom meant by the heart?"

Sophie nodded, warm goosebumps rippling over her skin. "The heartwood was the *beginning* of the tree. It's been there since the tree first started growing. It's the strongest part, too."

"Would you like that, Mom?" he said. "If they make a sculpture so you can keep the heart of the tree?"

His mother reached over and patted Craig and Sophie's hands.

"Well, that's what I walked all the way down here for, son. You're right, Sophie. The heart is the strongest. When can Mary get started on my sculpture?"

Now Sophie was fighting back tears, but she nodded and smiled.

"Just as soon as you decide what you want it to look like."

CHAPTER 7

The gigantic bonfire that marked the end of the Lightning Gap Harvest Festival and the true turning of the seasons was spectacular to behold. Donations from Sophie and her family along with other people who came from all around created a warm, fragrant blaze more than ten feet high, with swirling, dancing sparks soaring at least twice as far above.

Mugs of hot apple cider for the kids and spiked versions for some of the adults made the rounds. What had to be the entire town and a few hundred more stood or sat in the circle, and the fire itself was louder than the low whispers of conversation.

Every few minutes, someone would walk up to the fire and toss a small bundle in. Sophie explained those were pieces of paper wrapped around scrap wood. Every one with a drawing or writing or whatever people wanted to give to the fire that year.

Or to wish for in the year to come.

Somehow the quiet, thoughtful crowd felt every bit as exciting to Craig.

As for himself, in that moment he couldn't think of a thing in the world to wish for.

Mrs. Holbrook had bundled up his father after all once the scare was over, and the three of them sat cozy together at his side. A couple of the sheriffs had suggested local groups who could help him a bit more, with people who were prepared and trained for the new trouble his mother was having.

In the back of his mind, he suspected having the incredible carving that rested against his knees at the house would solve that problem. But he wanted a bit more time to himself going forward.

Or more honestly, time with Sophie, as much as he could manage.

She sat close beside him, her leg and shoulder warm against his. He still felt that connection sparking between them, but even with so much fire, he didn't feel that damaging intensity. He knew that might change over time as it had with his other lovers.

But he had the strangest feeling this time the spark between them wouldn't get hot enough to burn itself out.

The carving itself was about three feet across

and several inches thick, and he kept wanting to touch it to make sure it wasn't a real sunflower. The petals and seeds stood out in unbelievable detail, and Mary had promised to show him how to stain the seeds with linseed oil to keep them dark and smooth.

He was looking forward to how the rest would weather and crack and warp—and grow even more beautiful—over time.

Just like people did.

CANINE Cupid

JASON A. ADAMS

To Golly,
whose approval helped me win Kari's heart.

CHAPTER 1

$\mathcal{N}$othing's lonelier than sitting alone at work on Christmas Eve.

Through the window, Diane Stumbaugh watched a few half-hearted snowflakes blowing around in the light from the parking lot streetlamp. The road outside was deserted. The last airplane of the night had landed two hours ago at the little regional airport across the way. The lobby of the emergency vet clinic was silent, except for her own breathing. Even the kennels, usually full of barking and yowling animals, were empty for a change.

Her only company was a row of chairs, chrome and black vinyl sentinels guarding the sunny linoleum floor and eggshell walls. A bowl of miniature Reese's Cup trees sat in a bowl on the counter, lonely and sad. Posters of dog and cat breeds, parrots with (not really) funny speech balloons, and fee charts hung here and there. A wire rack sat near the glass doors, full of helpful brochures on such thrilling subjects as dental care for cats, heartworm preventatives for dogs, how to keep your budgie healthy.

Diane managed to kill half an hour rearranging the pamphlets for best effect.

Twice.

She'd turned the TV off hours ago. She couldn't stand the relentless parade of Christmas feel-good on every channel. She *could* sweep and mop the floors again, but her nose still burned from the stink of antiseptic cleaner from the last time.

Maybe she should call Charlotte.

No, the idea of talking to her ex, of being so desperate that the only person she could reach out to was the woman who'd tossed her out like last week's garbage...

Enough of that.

Diane got up, stretched, and went to the break room to brew a cup of Swiss Miss and maybe nuke some popcorn. A glance at her watch told her the shift would last two and a half more hours. She'd still have the on-call pager, but at least she could go home after that.

Back to her empty apartment, still full of empty places where someone else's things should be.

At least she had a new bottle of Angel's Envy

bourbon out in the car. She could give Santa an expensive toast if he decided to show up.

Two hours later, she'd finished three more cups of cocoa. She hung up her white coat and stethoscope, and switched out her lime-green scrubs for a plain white tank top and red running shorts. The snow was getting thicker outside. Thank goodness she had warmer clothes with her.

She was pulling a dingy pair of gray sweatpants out of her backpack when the office phone buzzed like a pissed-off hornet in a megaphone.

Diane immediately switched from brooding, lonely whiner to doctor mode. She dropped the sweats and jogged to the phone. As much as she hated when animals were suffering, she finally had something to *do*.

"Tri-Cities Emergency Animal Hospital, Dr. Stumbaugh speaking."

CHAPTER 2

Katie Rogers threw her cell phone on the passenger seat and sped through the deepening snow. In the rear seat, her German Shepherd mix gave another of those jaw-splitting hacks, like she was trying to cough out her own back feet. A sharp smell of urine filled the car.

"Hang on, Golly girl! Almost there!"

She urged the car faster, even though the tires were starting to slip in the curves. The headlights tried to pierce the snow, but the view through the windshield was like the *Millennium Falcon* going into hyperdrive.

And there it was. Katie barely saw the glowing white sign for the animal hospital. She certainly couldn't read the lettering through the swirling snowflakes, but the stylized black cat and dog were big enough to recognize.

She cut the wheel sharply, sending the little Civic into a short skid. Fortunately, enough sand and ice had overflowed from the street, and the tires grabbed hold.

She slid to a stop, the car at an awkward angle to the glass doors. She turned the key and jumped out, just as a short, ebony-haired woman in a lab coat came running through the door, pushing a shiny steel cart.

"Thank you. Oh, thank you thank you for being here," Katie said, yanking open the rear door. "She's back here. Please hurry!" She ignored the sharp wind biting through the thin flannel of her favorite pajamas. At least she'd thought to put on her rubber snow boots and poofy winter jacket.

The vet hurried to her side, and together they managed to get the eighty-five pound Golly onto the cart, where she gave another of those heaving, heart-breaking gags. Damp snow lashed Katie's face and got in her eyes, mixing with her frightened tears.

"Hold the door," Dr. Stumbaugh said in a tone worthy of any first-grade teacher. "I've got her. We're going straight back to the first exam room, on the left."

Katie waited until the cart was through the outer door, then rushed past to open the door the vet pointed to. They got Golly in the room, and then onto the brushed steel exam table.

"She got in the trash, and the coughing started shortly after, correct?"

"Yes, that's right," Katie said, petting Golly's head and stroking her ears. "I don't think there were any chemicals or anything in there, but she's been like this for nearly half an hour now."

Dr. Stumbaugh took a penlight from her breast pocket and tried to look in Golly's mouth, but the big baby struggled too much.

"She's a little frightened," the doctor said in a low, soothing voice. "Understandable, given how uncomfortable she must be. I'm going to give her something to calm her down, if you can just hold her foreleg still."

Katie gripped Golly's leg, tears running down her face as her baby panted and heaved.

"It's okay, Golly. Mommy's here. Dr. Stumbaugh is going to make you all better."

"That's right," said the vet in her calm, slow voice. "Don't you worry, Miss Golly. Now just relax…"

She took a vial and syringe from a cabinet, drew a half-inch of clear liquid, then injected the struggling dog just above the elbow. Ten seconds later, Golly went limp. Her eyes were still open, but unfocused. Her head hit the table with a soft thump, and her long pink tongue flopped out of her mouth.

"Don't worry," Dr. Stumbaugh said, ruffling

Golly's ears. "She's fine. Just good and stoned. Can you hold her jaws apart, please?"

Katie couldn't help but calm down. Something about the vet's easy manner now that her patient wasn't under stress anymore. Katie's shoulders finally started to loosen their knots.

Dr. Stumbaugh shone the light into Golly's mouth, her other hand moving the dog's tongue this way and that.

"Ah hah! Thought so. Keep her mouth open, I'll be right back."

She left the room and Katie heard a metallic rattling, like someone dropping silverware in the sink. The vet came back in, holding a foot-long pair of forceps. She'd wrapped some sort of foam tape around the jaws.

"Don't worry," she said again. Katie realized her horror at the sight of the wicked implement must've showed. "Your pup's going to be just fine. How was the chicken dinner?"

"What? I don't—" Katie started, but stopped when Dr. Stumbaugh stuck the forceps down Golly's throat, wiggled them around for a couple of seconds, then carefully withdrew a small, jagged bone.

"There we are. She'll be just fine, Ms. Rogers. She probably would've coughed it up or swallowed it down eventually, but they can scare you to death when they start coughing like that. I'll want to keep her here for a bit, see how she does when she wakes up, but I'd say that by morning you won't even know anything happened."

"Thank you so *so* much!" Katie said, throwing her arms around the shorter woman and kissing her cheek. "I can't tell you how much I appreciate you."

"Just doing my job." Diane tried not to let her fluster show. "Why don't we go wait in the break room, after you hang up your jacket? I don't think either of us will be going anywhere until the plows and salt trucks come back through, anyway. I make a mean hot chocolate, and we can raid the Reese's Cups from the waiting area."

"Oh my God, I *love* reesie cups!"

CHAPTER 3

*D*iane guided Golly's hoomun to the tiny break room and got her settled down at the tiny formica table. Now that the excitement was over and Golly was going to be okay, the woman's hands shook with adrenaline and relief.

She could finally see the *person*, and not the emergency. Katie Rogers was a little taller than Diane, and had a Rubenesque figure and rosy, cherubic face. Thick hair the color of burnt oak hung down to her shoulders. Huge blue eyes and thick, full lips that made for an amazing smile.

The plaid flannel PJs were just adorable.

Diane should stay on the cautious side, but it was nearly Christmas. Snow was piling up outside. Surely she'd been good enough this year.

"Well, we've got a few hours, Ms. Rogers.

Might as well get to know each other. How long have you had Miss Golly?"

"Nearly eight years, since she was only a couple months old," she said, blowing on her cocoa, lips smudged at the corner with chocolate and faux peanut butter. "Please, call me Katie."

Diane unbuttoned her lab coat and sat down across from Katie.

"Only if you call me Diane, Katie. That's a pretty name." She saw Katie staring, and looked down.

And blushed. She'd forgotten she was only wearing the thin tank and shorts. She started to close her coat, then thought what the hell? It's only the two of us in here.

"Sorry for the not-so-professional attire," she said. "I was just changing to go home when you called."

"No, I'm the one that's sorry," Katie said. "I hate that we're keeping you from your family on Christmas Eve."

"Don't worry. I don't have any family, at least not close by. That's why I'm working tonight."

"Oh." Katie sipped her cocoa and they sat in a comfortable, uncomfortable silence.

"How about you?" Diane asked. "Anyone at home besides our girl in there?"

"No, just me and her." Katie sighed. "There

was…well, never mind. Less said about that the better."

"Please don't tell me there's a Mr. Rogers."

They both laughed at what to Katie was probably a *very* moldy old joke.

"Just my dad, thank goodness."

Diane liked her laugh. A lot. It was free and open, unfettered by false decorum. Maybe it was Christmas Eve, maybe it was the situation. Maybe it was that laugh. Something made her feel bolder than usual.

"Say, Katie. Would you be uncomfortable if I shuck this silly white coat? Polyester and bare legs don't mix very well."

"It's your house. Make yourself at home." A little smile played around the chocolaty corners of her mouth. "I don't mind telling you, I was worried sick, and now I could use something a little stronger than cocoa."

"I can prescribe something for that," Diane said with a chuckle. "Just let me run out to the car."

CHAPTER 4

Katie almost forget where she was and why.

Several sips of excellent whiskey had banished the chill and the nervous shakes. She felt completely relaxed, in spite of the surroundings. Golly now slept on a pile of towels on the break room floor, curled up and snoring softly between their feet.

Diane was wonderful company. She kept Katie laughing with stories about animals and owners, about her Tennessee childhood, and about all the trouble she'd gotten in as a kid with her rambunctious brothers.

She was also *awfully* easy on the eyes. She had the cutest little crooked mouth that showed dainty little teeth every time she smiled. She had a runner's long legs, but wasn't all skinny and lanky like so many jogger types. Muscles rippled every time she moved her fair-skinned arms, and Katie remembered how easily Diane'd lifted her gynormous dog down from the exam table and carried her to break room.

A loud rumble from outside marked the passage of the first snowplow of the day. She and Diane had talked the whole night away. Katie hadn't felt so free and easy with anyone for a long, long time.

Under the table, Golly snorted, then smacked her lips just like Katie's dad used to do when he woke up in the mornings.

"Hey, girlie-girl. You finally awake, sleepy head?" Katie reached down and felt a soft, warm tongue lick her hand. "Silly old thing. You need to say thank you to Dr. Stumbaugh here."

Golly crawled out from under the table, yawned, and gave a huge stretch, head down and butt high. Then she surprised the hell out of Katie by walking over to Diane and giving her hand a lick or two. She usually took quite a while to warm up to new people.

"Yesh, you's a good girl," Diane said, using both hands to waller Golly's ears, her face right down in the dog's. "You's a good, big, silly girl. No more gettin' in the trash, 'kay?"

Golly grunted and groaned and licked the vet's face, coating her with slobber. Katie was horrified, but Diane just laughed and pulled a couple of paper towels from the roll on the wall.

"I think someone's feeling ready to go home," she said. "I also think that's a fine idea. I know *I'm* beat."

Go home? Suddenly Katie thought that sounded like a grand idea, but not just yet. And maybe not alone. She reached across and grabbed Diane's hand.

"Listen...um...candy or not, I'm still kinda hungry. I know it's Christmas Day and all, but I bet IHOP's open. Want to join me? It's my treat. Since you don't have any family gatherings, maybe we could catch a movie later? I don't know what's playing but..."

She snapped her mouth closed, aware she was babbling like she always did when nervous or shy. Or after a few shots of good bourbon.

But Diane just looked at her. She didn't take her hand back, and a smile slowly spread across her face.

At their feet, Golly gave an impatient "voof." American dogs say *woof*, but German dogs say *voof*.

Stop it, Katie! Don't make a fool out of yourself.

"You know what?" Diane said, gripping Katie's hand more tightly and pulling her closer. "I think pancakes and movies sounds like a *fantastic* way to spend Christmas. But let's not leave Miss Golly here out of it."

Diane drew her closer yet, and Katie closed her eyes when she felt Diane's lips on hers, sending heat through her belly and shivers down her spine. An endless second later, Diane pulled back.

"I have all the claymation Christmas specials on DVD at my place, and Golly's more than welcome to the sofa. I can make us some pancakes and bake up some of my special carob dog treats for the girl. You can even wear your jammies. What do you say?"

Katie couldn't stop the grin that stretched her cheeks. She hugged Golly's savior as hard as she could and whispered in Diane's soft ear.

"I say Merry Christmas, Diane. And I think it's going to be one hell of a Happy New Year."

Happily Ever After In Krampus Land

KARI KILGORE

AUTHOR OF MORNING GLORY AND THE SWEETEST TROUBLE

For Jason

Who survived the glorious madness
of the Nineties with me

HAPPILY EVER AFTER IN KRAMPUSLAND

November first had long been Thom Metzger's favorite day of the year.

Sure, he was sad Halloween was over like most other folks he knew. The costumes, the candy, the parties. Childhood pleasures of trick-or-treating and sugar buzz giving way to elaborate adult costume contests and spooky cocktails bubbling away with slivers of dry ice.

The general air of everyone who felt a bit strange—a bit out of place for the rest of the year— celebrating one night when people *wanted* to be more like them.

The netherworldly decorations at Janson Park, the local amusement park, had been Thom's favorite part since he was one of the little kids squealing and collecting candy. The silly, kind of tired and worn down Seventies amusement park normally featured pastel decorations and old matte paintings of landscapes that didn't look real anymore once you turned ten.

But that all changed when summer gave way to autumn.

Jimmy Howard, the owner of Janson Park for the last fifteen years, spent much more on eerie backdrops, lighting, and employee costumes for Halloween and other holidays than on anything for the kiddies. October brought in a heck of a lot more money than the good-enough-to-get-by totals for the spring and summer seasons combined.

Especially after dark. When admission was twenty-one and older only, and guests happily paid for overpriced drinks and all the specialty chocolates in every shape, size, and variation. Some of those special designs could still bring an old-fashioned childhood blush to Thom's face.

Only December was a bigger, busier month for Janson Park.

Tonight was the last Halloween-themed fling, with a massive King and Queen of the Night parade through the black and orange, bat and cat-dominated wonderland to close up the season with style. Thom waited in the near-midnight chill at the end of the parade route through the park, shivering along with everyone else who would get to work the second the gates were locked behind the last departing guest. He wished he'd had time for one more cup of Mr. Howard's fantastic pre-shift hot chocolate.

Whatever the boss spiked it with for the end-of-season festivities kept Thom warm on the inside, at least for a little while.

The dreary backstage area never changed all year long. Same faded, cracked concrete, full of ridges and valleys from almost fifty years of winters and summers in the north Georgia mountains. Same unpainted plywood and plaster backs of fake buildings, revealing how cheap and fast the original construction had been.

Ghouls, goblins, vampires, and every other manner of Halloween spirit flounced, danced, or twirled through the multi-colored fog bank obscuring the open gate. The second they were out of sight of the last yelling and cheering guests, they all reverted to a weary plod, dragging off their masks and gowns and capes.

Nothing but sweaty, tired humans, every one.

When Mr. Howard first let Thom work at Janson Park when he was fifteen, a still-little-boy part of him worried about seeing too much behind the scenes. Knowing how all the magic of every season came to life. But over the last six years, he'd only come to love each redecoration of the park even more.

What Thom loved most about the first of

November was what typical people were sad about as summer passed further into memory. The focus of Janson Park and the town that had grown up around it turned from colorful autumn to long, cold winter.

For Thom, that meant the transformation into KrampusLand.

A thrill of anticipation shivered up his spine. More than the thought of finally being part of the only festival better than Halloween lit up his nerves and raised the hairs on his neck and arms.

A rising surge of crowd noise let him and everyone else know the parade was coming to an end.

The Queen of the Night in her horseless carriage could only be next.

Otherwise known as Julie Howard, Thom's best friend since she'd moved here when they were both in first grade.

What looked like a round black cage slowly passed through the billowing veil of purple, green, and red clouds. Several menacing footmen walked alongside, all of them dressed in blood-red uniforms and wearing remarkably lifelike red devil masks. The metal bars and glass windows of the carriage sparkled with iridescence, highlighting the glorious vision inside. Julie sat on a miniature throne that glittered as if it were made out of black ice.

Her ball gown and crown matched the red of her

footmen, and made her porcelain-pale skin and curly raven black hair even more beautiful. She grinned at Thom now, but he knew she'd held her face cold and regal when anyone who'd paid to get into Janson Park that night could see her.

The carriage slowed to a halt, and Thom stepped up to the front without a whole lot of hassle. Several of the other guys and a few of the girls who worked the Halloween season would have been happy to help the Queen of the Night step back down into reality. Not to mention getting close to the daughter of the park's owner.

Thom couldn't help but feel a flush of pride that they respected his years of friendship with Julie enough to back off.

He tried to ignore the flutter of hope that she might want him for more than friendship someday. That flutter had been with him more and more over the last couple of months.

Julie raised her voice over the cheers and applause from inside the park.

"What a crowd!" She took Thom's hand as she stepped out of the carriage. "I don't think one more person could have packed in here tonight."

Thom tried not to giggle at the bright pink sneakers poking out from under the ball gown.

One of the frightful footmen stood on Julie's other side, booted feet wide apart, muscled arms crossed. Even through the distraction of the high, brick-red cheekbones and heavy black eyebrows of his mask, blue eyes clearly focused on Thom's hand holding Julie's, then on Thom's face.

Jimmy Howard. Julie's father, of course. And Thom's boss.

Thom let go of her hand before he was ready.

"Biggest crowd we've ever had outside of December," Mr. Howard said. His booming voice normally had no trouble cutting through any kind of racket, but he spoke low enough for only Julie and Thom. "Everyone's gonna have to haul ass to top this month, but with what I've got planned for December, I'm pretty sure we'll manage."

Mr. Howard pulled out his smartphone, and started to raise it so he could see past his demonic cheekbones. He snorted and pulled the mask off instead. Hair the same black as Julie's stood up all over his head, except where it had retreated from the corners. A few taps on the phone, and the gates standing open into the backstage area moved toward the interior of the park.

Lumpy gray stone that looked surprisingly authentic tonight passed through the billowing clouds, leaving only a squared-off frame of yellowing pine in its wake. The cloud machines cut off, sending one last burst of color spiraling up into the overhead lights.

Julie's pre-recorded announcement started up over the loudspeakers.

"Thank you all for attending another spooktacular month of HalloweenLand here at Janson Park. We're glad you survived! Mark your calendars and join us starting the Saturday after Thanksgiving for the magic of HolidayLand. And return for the nighttime thrills and chills of KrampusLand, if you dare..."

The announcement continued, reminding everyone it would be safe to bring the kiddies for daytime holiday cheer with Santa and all the elves. Then to come back after dark for adults-only fun, when Krampus would reward them for being nice.

And reward them even more if they were naughty.

More adults than Thom or anyone else would have believed five years ago were delighted to take their chances to make it onto the naughty list.

Thom raised his eyebrows at Julie. "*Spook*tacular?"

She rolled her eyes and jerked her thumb at her father.

"He writes this stuff, not me. *And* he has to pay me for my time to record it."

"I haven't paid you for anything just yet, smartass."

Mr. Howard glanced around the milling crowd. That was enough to get most of them moving. The return of his booming voice sent everyone into double-time.

"All right, get to it. Get all this parade junk back in storage and sweep up out in the park. A crew's coming in first thing in the morning to tear down HalloweenLand. We're all back here at two o'clock sharp to start turning this dump into a freakin' winter wonderland."

The second Mr. Howard walked toward the huge storage barns at the back of the lot, Julie grabbed Thom's hand again. Thick fake eyelashes and way too much red lipstick looked bizarre up close, but the smirk was pure Julie.

"I've got to get out of Evil Cinderella's getup before my face freezes this way. See you tomorrow for the usual post-Halloween chocolate binge?"

Every change in the season, especially the winter holidays and the major candy fests like Valentine's Day and Easter, someone had to deal with all the leftover chocolate goodies that no one would want to buy any more. Hearts and cupids (and the modern, more anatomically correct accessories brought in especially for February 14) were depressing by the time the Easter Bunny hopped into town. A bit creepy, too.

Same with the bunnies that didn't quite fit in once the May Day festivities got started, and the ones no one wanted to share with their children. Thom thought chocolate rabbits brazenly engaged in the act of making more rabbits really *should* have worked all spring long.

So when they were kids, Julie always shared what she could get away with bringing to school. Thom had later joined in the employees-only chocolate binge for the less family-friendly variety.

Mr. Howard never minded the expense. He privately said since the sugar buzz got the park cleaned up and transformed in record time, it was worth every penny.

And now Julie's hand was warm and soft in Thom's, driving away all traces of the chilly night. His unruly brain and other parts of him declared he'd go anywhere and do anything if it meant spending time with her.

He hoped his smile wasn't too wide or goofy.

"I'll be there. I'd never be mean enough to leave you on your own with an unreasonable amount of chocolate."

UNLIKE HALLOWEENLAND, which was mostly a big party, every inch of the park had to be polished and perfect for HolidayLand. Pretty much as long as booze and snacks were available and restrooms were clean, October visitors were happy. Give them a couple of creepy or adult HalloweenLand trinkets to show off to their friends (creating a massive free advertising campaign for the park), and they returned year after year.

Not so in December. Weirdoes and normal folks alike had money to spend and merry to make, and the park had to get ready for all of them.

Thom had helped clean, stock, and redecorate all the gift shops before, amazed at the sheer volume of gifts, souvenirs, and memorabilia guests wanted to buy and take back home with them. The usual crew could manage to get it done in a few weeks if all of them pushed extra hard.

Their only break between the first of November and opening night was a couple of days off for Thanksgiving. Thom was even more thankful than usual that he'd spend those days with Julie's family, same as the last few years.

Everything holiday-related that Thom could imagine and more packed the shelves in the all-day shops. Figurines and ornaments of Santa and everything that went with him, countless styles of menorahs and dreidels, and hard-to-find decorations and symbols for winter festivals all over the world. The cheapest stocking stuffer shared space with clothing and jewelry that cost more than Thom's car.

The shops that didn't open until after the sun went down were stuffed just as full of every possible variety of Krampus and the Green Man and the Grinch, along with rather grownup depictions of holiday cheer.

Imported European booze-flavored and filled chocolates shared space with pourable and paintable varieties, but Thom's favorites were even more specialized.

Each year, HolidayLand offered a different limited-edition flavor, made up for that season and so far never repeated. A bizarre but unforgettable list of ingredients got blended with whatever chocolate suited them best.

Camel's milk, shitake mushroom, absinthe, and even juniper chocolates were made into truffles, wrapped in festive foil paper, or added into hot drinks for visitors who waited in line however long it took to get them.

As Mr. Howard never tired of saying, all of that potential profit required dressing the whole park up in its holiday best.

Miles of silver, gold, red, and green garland. Gigantic wreaths made of ornaments and bells along with the traditional green and red on every doorway. Ornate, glittering stars half as tall as Thom hanging everywhere they could possibly fit. Truckloads of flowers and greenery, poinsettias and holly as far as the eye could see lining the trails and pathways.

Even the restrooms were scrubbed and fresh-smelling and festive.

This year, for the first time, Thom wasn't part of all of the typical holiday madness out in the park. He admitted to himself, and no one else, that he kind of missed the scent of peppermint and pine that took over every corner of the place. He even missed unpacking and shelving all those new trinkets, just a little.

Like most of the crew that worked the winter holidays, Thom didn't have any family close by. He'd been a late-life surprise baby, so his own parents were gone. Imagining the guests taking everything they bought home to their own families had always kept him cheery all the way through New Year's Eve.

That and spending the off-days with Julie and her father, their swarms of visiting aunts, uncles, and plenty of kiddies running around.

Working in the warehouse on the back lot, getting the KrampusLand costumes and decorations ready, turned out to be a heck of a lot more fun than stocking the gift shops. And every bit as busy.

Best of all, Halloween's demonic masks paled in comparison to the Krampus hordes. Instead of red and smooth, these masks were weathered shades of blue, grey, and brown that needed touching up every year and often during the season.

Deep wrinkles and knobbly horns, sometimes two or more pairs per mask, needed dusting.

No footmen's uniforms here that could go to the dry cleaner, either. Each Krampus beast would sport monstrous, ragged fur, and carry staffs, bundles of switches, or gigantic brass bells. Every bit of it hand-made and hand-maintained.

All the better to rampage through the nighttime streets of KrampusLand, terrorizing and delighting guests and employees alike.

The gossip was certainly better in the warehouse, with word of Mr. Howard's extra-special surprise getting around at light speed. No one seemed to know exactly *what* he'd arranged on his and Julie's trips to Europe back in the spring, but he'd hinted more than once that it would be big. So the tales flew hot and furious, each speculating a wilder and more frightening version of the boss's secretive deal with the original Krampus demon.

Julie only smiled and shook her head when people asked her for details, over and over and over again. Her smile wore a bit thin by the middle of November.

Thom hadn't quite worked up the nerve to bring it up himself when she tapped his shoulder one afternoon, glancing from side to side like a cartoon villain. He gladly set aside the bundle of switches he was working on. Weaving black and silver ribbon through so they'd hold together *and* allow each Krampus to pull one out for a swat was much harder than it looked.

"What's up, Madame Perchta?"

Julie blew out air through her lips, straight up and hard enough to lift the black curls off of her forehead.

"Cut it out, Thom, or you can go right back to

your bundle. My father's grand idea of me dressing up as *Fraulein* Perchta isn't quite as bad as making me go as the wrinkled old lady version, but it's close. Perchta wasn't the only thing we brought back from the Europe trips. Get over here!"

Thom stood and stretched, hands pressed against the small of his back. He'd been sitting there hunched over a table full of piles of branches and spools of ribbon longer than he'd realized. He followed Julie around the corner and out of the main warehouse, unable to resist a quick glance over his shoulder. No one was looking his way.

Julie walked so fast down the dim hallway that Thom had to almost run to catch up. Beautiful as her Queen of the Night gown had been, and as her sparkling white Perchta dress would surely be, he preferred her in an old sweatshirt and faded blue jeans.

Everyone in the warehouse wore pretty much the same, including Thom. But no one looked nearly as good in them as Julie did.

"Can you keep a secret?" she said, leaning close enough that Thom caught the faint, intoxicating scent of her spice and roses perfume. "Well, two secrets, but one really big."

"That depends. Is one of them the chocolate for the season?"

Julie let out a great, glorious laugh, and Thom

was delighted to see the sweetest blush in the world move across her pale cheeks.

"Now I'm not so sure I want to show you after all."

Julie stopped and leaned against the wall with her arms crossed (but looking about a thousand times cuter than her father in the same pose). She turned her head and stared up at the ceiling, but Thom caught the way her lips twitched, fighting off a grin.

He leaned against the wall beside her, shoulder to shoulder, hip to hip. The same way they'd sat or stood countless times over the years. But the warmth of her body, the curve of her flesh, got every bit of Thom's attention in a way it never had before.

"Come on, Julie. Who else you gonna show besides me? Secrets you keep to yourself lose half their fun."

She giggled and leaned her head on his shoulder. He hoped she didn't notice the way he held his breath, hoping she'd stay right there forever.

"Well, okay. If you put it that way. Come on."

She darted into the first door on the right, into a room Thom had never been inside before. It looked like an ordinary break room, with a row of ordinary white kitchen cabinets, a sink, a microwave, and a coffee maker. A few chairs around a plain pine table and a white refrigerator completed the cheapest-stuff-at-the-warehouse look of the place.

But the *smell*...

Thom breathed in, closing his eyes at the rich scent of dark chocolate, good coffee, and something he couldn't quite identify.

"Sit," Julie said, standing beside one of the cabinets. "And cover your eyes."

Thom made a show of rolling his eyes instead, but he sat and promptly put both hands over his face like a little boy. Leaving his mouth exposed, of course.

He heard Julie opening the cabinet, then rustling and the soft thump of something hitting the table in front of him. He breathed in again and smiled.

Two of his favorite things in the world.

Chocolate and Julie standing close to him.

"Okay," she said. "Open up and brace yourself for heaven."

Thom opened his mouth, doing his best to keep from imagining what heaven in a room along with Julie would really be like. A small bit of chocolate not much bigger than a Hershey's Kiss landed on his tongue.

On the savory side, almost like a Mexican mole sauce, but undoubtedly fine dark chocolate. And in the middle, the thick, creamy tang of...

"Cheese? You're putting chocolate with *cheese* this year?"

He opened his eyes, and Julie was grinning as she popped one of the chocolates into her own mouth.

"Isn't it divine? That's a truffle brie, which is unbelievably good on its own. But with the chocolate?" She rolled her eyes closed and sighed.

"You know, it works better than it has any right to," Thom said. "How do you two always come up with these things, year after year?"

Julie winked and pushed another small chocolate sitting in a sparkling red foil his way.

"It's a gift. The combinations, I mean. That and dad looks for this stuff all year long. Try that one. It's more for the kids, and for people not brave enough to try the cheese."

Thom popped it into his mouth, noticing right away the chocolate was much fruitier and sweeter. And the inside was fizzing more than even champagne could have.

"You got me on this one," he said, laughing. "It can't possibly be Pop Rocks, can it? Because that's what people who aren't brave enough to try the other one deserve, right? Something even stranger!"

Julie nodded, leaning sideways toward him into a fit of giggles like she had since she was a little girl. Thom couldn't help but join her. Once they finally managed to catch their breath, he bowed, pretending to sweep his non-existent hat off.

"I thank you, madame, for sharing your two

wondrous secrets with me. I will take them to my grave. Or at least until opening day of Holi-dayLand."

"No, that was just *one*," Julie said. "Come on, the other one is even better."

They dashed down the hall again, with Julie refusing to say another word until she stopped by a window at the end of the hall, peeking through the slats of the plastic blinds. The gray and cloudy sky outside didn't let in much light.

When she turned, Julie's eyes glowed enough to make up for it.

"They're finally here," she said, her voice excited but quiet, even though they were alone. "Daddy's big surprise."

Thom stood shoulder to shoulder beside her again, breathing in the earthy scent of her hair now, thinking how glad he was the window was so small. Until he got a look outside.

Then he couldn't think anything at all.

He couldn't breathe, either.

Several huge trucks were parked out there, each with the biggest horse trailers Thom had ever seen tucked up behind them. They were all solid matte black, nearly as tall as the backs of the semis that flew along the interstate at terrifying speed, at least when compared to the tiny junker of a car Thom drove.

Walking slowly out of those trailers were gigantic, equally terrifying horses.

They were as black as the trailers, but the low light gleamed off of every sleek contour and bulging muscle. Thom didn't want to guess, didn't want to accept that such creatures could possibly be real.

But somewhere in the back of his reeling mind, he was sure they had to be seven feet tall at the shoulder. At least.

Thom's shuddering thoughts took over from there.

And their heads were huge and their teeth were sharp and their eyes would gleam red and fierce when the light hit them at night, when they stared him down right before they ran *him down.*

"Big surprise," he managed to whisper. "I'll say. Where did they *come* from?"

If Julie had noticed Thom's muscles rigid with fear, she showed no signs of it. Her voice was every bit as excited and vibrant as before.

"We found them in Europe. The woman who raised them said they're an English breed, Shire or something like that. But these came from Austria, up in the mountains. She should be out there somewhere, she's a real trip herself. Aren't they just *beautiful*, Thom?"

Thom blinked, realizing his eyes were as dry as

his throat. He turned toward toward Julie. Her cheeks were flushed again, and a smile lit her face. Even more so than when she was eating the fabulous secret chocolate, he'd never seen her quite so…radiant.

She was actually glad those massive beasts were there.

"What are… Why are they here?"

"For the parades, of course. They'll be part of the closing parade every night. I don't love the idea of dressing up as lily-white Perchta and having to act like a female Krampus, rampaging through the park and threatening everyone. Well, the threatening and rampaging part will probably be a lot of fun. But if I get to close out every night riding one of those gorgeous creatures, it will all be worth it."

She turned to Thom, but he knew she didn't really see him. After all their years of friendship, countless hours of joy and excitement and fear and sorrow, she would have noticed his clenched jaw and clammy skin if she'd been paying attention.

Julie was dazzled by those awful things outside.

Or maybe she had something else on her mind. Her blue eyes were still huge and bright.

"I get to choose who rides with me, Thom. It's not like the Queen and King of the Night thing, when we have separate carriages and don't even talk to each other. None of this is exactly traditional in Austria or anywhere else, but you know dad never worries too much about any of that."

She took Thom's hand, along with what little breath he'd managed to regain.

"I talked him into it. Into Perchta having a companion. Besides Krampus, I mean." She shuddered and shook her head, sending the curls floating over her shoulders. "I want *you* to ride with me."

Thom forced himself to swallow, trying not to wince at the dry click. Forcing himself to think wasn't much easier.

Had she just…

Did she just ask him to…

"You want me to ride with you? In the parade?"

She smiled and squeezed his hand, stepping closer.

"*Yeah*, in the parade. A bit more than that, I hope."

Thom's belly unfroze itself then, warming up and shooting sparks down his legs and up into his chest. His heart tried to whisper that she wasn't talking about the parade or the horses or anything else.

She was talking about *them*.

Thom and Julie. Julie and Thom.

And not just as friends, either.

But his mind, the old part that huddled in fear sometimes even though he had no idea why, kept throwing down waves of cold and resistance.

"You mean ride in a carriage, right?" he said. "Like for Halloween?"

Julie drew back and scowled for a second. Then her eyes widened, and Thom knew she'd finally gotten a good look at him. She took his other hand.

"I didn't mean in a carriage, no. I meant… Are you okay, Thom? What's wrong?"

He shook his head, trying to get the frigid wedge of fear to loosen its grip. The rest of his body was clamoring for his attention, and for Julie's.

"If you're saying what I think you're saying," he said, "that you want to, well, spend time with me, then I'm fine. *More* than fine. I can't think of anything I'd rather do, Julie."

He leaned forward and kissed her for a quick second. Now fireworks bigger and brighter and hotter than ten times what Janson Park shot on the Fourth of July blazed through his body.

But the fear didn't quite let go.

Julie's cheeks and throat were flushed now, and her pupils were huge.

But she still saw Thom like no one else ever had.

"Is it the horses?"

Thom risked a glance back outside. Twelve of the nightmare beasts stood together now, accepting apples and carrots from people who looked like children beside them. He kept waiting for one of them to shriek when a horse bit off their fingers or stomped on their feet.

"Yeah. The horses." He dragged a breath in and

held it for a second, trying to understand why he was talking about *this* when he'd just now, finally and at long last, kissed Julie. "I've never really been around them, not this close. I didn't expect to be this…afraid."

Julie didn't laugh or move away, and she didn't shake her head and frown, either.

She stepped forward and put her arms around him.

After a couple of shocked seconds, Thom did the same. Julie was warm and vibrant and fit him perfectly, as if she'd been designed for him. Or he'd been designed for her.

"You know what?" she said, her warm breath tickling his ear and thawing the block of ice in his brain a little more. "It doesn't matter. I don't care about that. It's *you* I care about, Thom. This was just my boneheaded way of letting you know."

Julie turned and kissed him then, and not a chaste, dainty kiss. She kissed him long and hard and deep, until Thom's mind and his heart and every other part of him thawed and melted and ran together into blissful oblivion.

He drew back, forcing air into his lungs for an entirely different reason. Before that blaze inside him could take over and wipe out his ability to think for a long, long time.

And this time, *Thom* really saw *Julie*.

Not the boss's daughter, or the gorgeous and

untouchable Queen of the Night. Not the icy and distant perfection of Perchta, and not a small amount of fear that went with her.

He saw the little girl with pigtails walking into class in first grade, scared to death showing up new in the middle of the school year. Sitting in the empty seat beside Thom instead of beside anyone else, flashing him a shy smile. Talking to him days later on the playground, telling him she'd just moved there with her daddy.

Tears running down her little girl cheeks when she whispered that her mommy had stayed where they'd come from.

That same girl years later, sitting with Thom at each of his parents' funerals. At their triumphs and failures, large and small. Through boyfriends and girlfriends, breakups and betrayals, always turning to each other in the end.

Thom held Julie's face in his hands, wondering how she'd look in five years, or ten. Or twenty or thirty or fifty.

He had no doubt she'd be every bit as beautiful as in this instant.

"Are you afraid of anything else?" she said, smiling. "Like me?"

Thom laughed. "I'm afraid of all kinds of things. And I'm *terrified* of you. But not nearly as much as I'm scared of those horses."

She kissed him again. Her lips were sweeter and

darker and saltier and spicier and a million times better than any chocolate in the whole world.

"I can work with that." Julie did step away then, reaching for his hand. "Come on, I'll introduce you. You don't have to get close until you're ready. I know they'll love you as much as I do."

Thom was too dazed, and too happy, to do anything but follow.

FIRST Kiss

JASON A. ADAMS

Author of *Canine Cupid* and *For the Love of Snarla Jane*

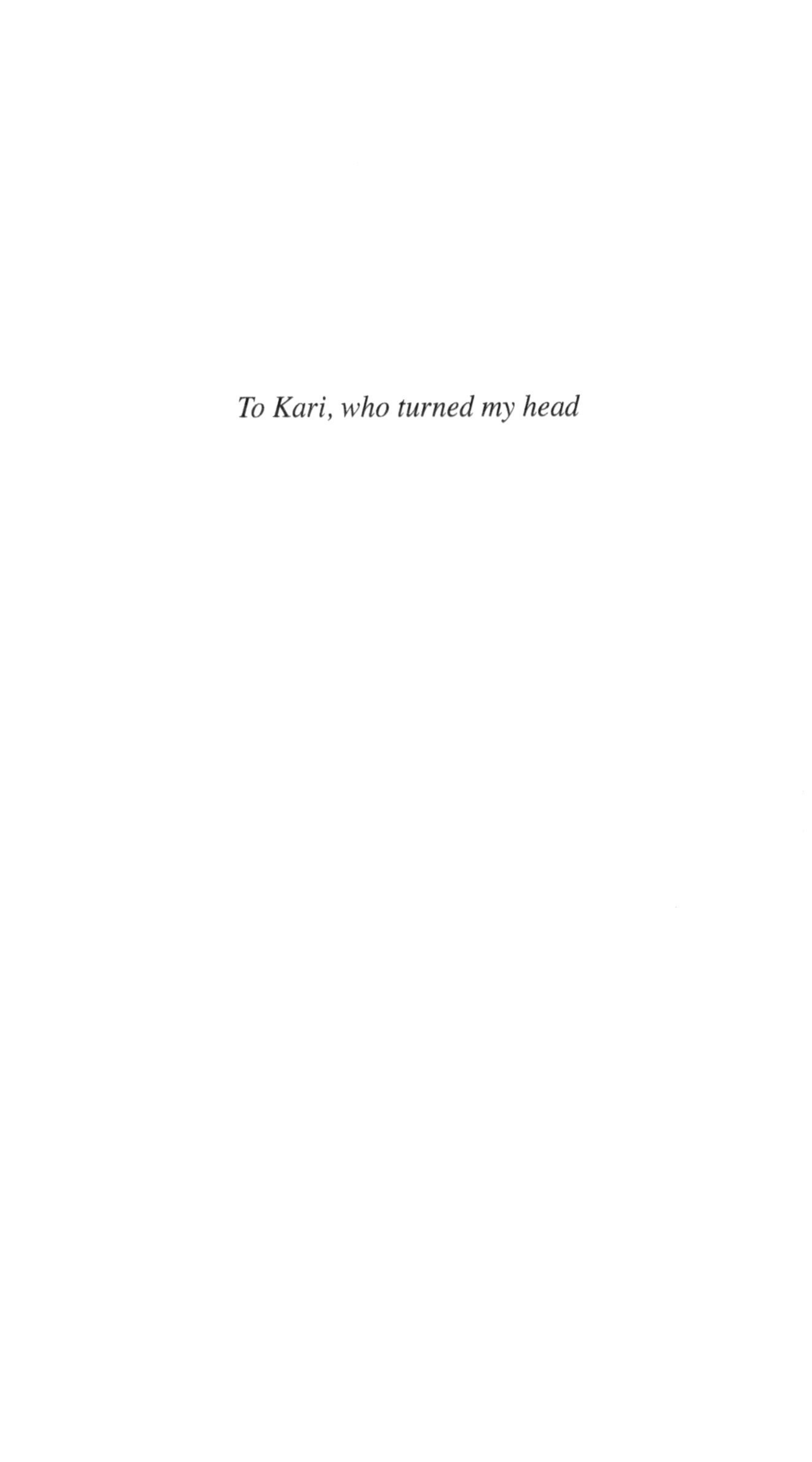

To Kari, who turned my head

CHAPTER 1

$\mathcal{A}$my Holbrook loved days like this.

The September sun still threw more warmth than she approved of, but the breeze carried the first nip of autumn. Days in the seventies and nights in the fifties. Cloudy skies and soft rains. No client interviews today, just a meeting with a computer contractor, so she got to wear her blue jeans and tartan flannel. Yay!

Up and down 4th Avenue, people strolled in and out of curio shops, delis and diners, and the now-ubiquitous camping supply stores. Most were locals on a Tuesday morning, but even during the week Holly Creek got a few folks from away. On the weekends, especially now that the forested ridges were dressing up in their fall colors of fiery reds, sunny yellows, and brilliant oranges, all the shops would be crammed with would-be mountaineers, here to bike or hike the Sugar Hill trails. All looking to take home some gin-yoo-wine Appalachian goodies.

She walked out of Sweetcakes Bakery carrying a large soy latte in one hand, and a wonderful buttermilk donut in the other. A donut that would cost her at least ten thousand steps today, but what the hell?

The little coffee shop was only one of several new businesses which had opened up in the no-longer-sleepy town of Estonoa, Virginia. Once derelict and facing the wrecking ball, most of the old brick buildings lining the three main streets had been lovingly renovated and refilled. Eateries, craft shops, live music on the hotel's lawn, even a new museum on the second floor of her own building.

Between good pastries and excellent tomato pie from the Railsong Hotel's new restaurant, breaks and lunches had certainly improved for the staff at the Holbrook law office.

She turned her head and closed her eyes as a couple of ATVs went roaring by on the dusty street. And sighed.

Unfortunately, the main thing driving the town's regrowth was the Arrowhead Trail system, a series of motorcycle, ATV, and UTV trails built on one of the long-abandoned strip mine sites. The town council in its infinite wisdom had decided to relax the ban on off-road vehicles inside town limits, and now their angry buzzing filled the air more often than not.

Add that to the grant the town had received to update the archaic water and sewer lines—which required tearing up every paved road in town for six months or more—and the result was a real mess.

But still, the old burg had new life. The population had stopped dropping and people had jobs. *Real* jobs. Jobs that didn't involve dying young from rockfalls, black lung, or any of the other ailments that went along with grubbing coal from the ground.

Amy checked both ways before crossing the street, a habit left over from her time in Atlanta. She'd gotten her BA in English Lit (*magna cum laude*, thank you very much) at Georgia Tech, then come back home to decide what to do next.

And ended up working in her uncle's law office. First as a legal assistant, then as a paralegal. She'd been bit by the law bug as she watched Uncle Jay not so much practice law, but rather do what he could to help the people in this small pocket of the mountains.

Wills, estates, and trusts to ease people's minds about the future. Fights with medical insurance companies that didn't want to pay out for broken miners and their families. Land disputes that he usually managed to settle with enough humor and fairness that once-raging neighbors left the office laughing and shaking hands.

Amy wanted to do that. To help people make things right. She had no interest in being a courtroom litigator, but she quickly mastered contract law, small-scale banking law, and real property law. Fortunately, Virginia still allowed *reading the law*, basically allowing a potential legal eagle to apprentice with an established attorney, instead of going through law school, and Uncle Jay was a fantastic, if merciless, instructor.

Uncle Jay was there when she received the letter from the Virginia Bar Association confirming her as Amy Holbrook, Esq., Attorney at Law. She wasn't sure which of them was more proud. He'd stayed on for a couple of years before retiring, making sure Amy knew not only the legal ropes, but how to run an office in a small town where all businesses were everybody's business.

Unfortunately, all the years spent with her nose to the grindstone hadn't done wonders for her social life. Which was fine. She had her work, her friends, and Bella the Pibble at home.

Her mom was always on her to get out, meet people. Mom wasn't getting any younger, as she endlessly reminded Amy. Who had no desire whatsoever to be the one supplying her mom's grandkiddie fix.

She opened the door to her uncle's—now hers,

she supposed—office. An old brass bell over the door dinged cheerily, and Amy smiled. The place wasn't much, just a few rooms on the bottom floor of an old clothing factory that now housed her and Bella's tiny upstairs apartment, the Holly Creek museum, and decades worth of her uncle's beloved files and antiques on the third floor.

But it was all hers. Uncle Jay had signed the building over to her, sneaking in a few superbly ridiculous clauses into the contract to see if she was on her toes.

She especially liked the one about promising to keep the bazoon in the attic fed and watered.

She set her coffee and donut down on the reception desk and checked her watch. The computer whiz should be here in fifteen minutes or so. Terri, the office little-bit-of-everything, should be back by then, but Amy would watch the desk just in case.

Besides, that donut wasn't going to eat itself.

Amy had just taken a huge bite of heaven when the brass bell over the door dinged again. And nearly choked when she saw her visitor.

He was flat out *gorgeous*. About her own five-eleven in height, broad shoulders pushing out a green-checked flannel shirt. Thick arms that ended in hands that looked like they could crush gravel. His shaggy auburn hair brushed the shirt's collar, and a full beard covered his face just below ruddy cheeks. A pair of Levis button flys barely contained what looked to be a fine pair of muscular legs.

Blue eyes sparkled at her between the shag and the beard as she desperately tried to swallow her mouthful.

"'Scuse me, miss. You go on now and finish eatin'. Don't worry none about me, I'll just wait a spell."

Dammit!

CHAPTER 2

ony Stanley drove slowly up Highway 58-A, staying in the right-hand lane so he could creep along and stare at the mountains.

Damn it felt fine to be back home!

After ten years in Atlanta, first at college and then working short-term contracts as he built up his computer and networking skills, he'd finally had enough. Enough of the crowds, the traffic, the noise… All of it.

At the ripe old age of thirty-five, he turned in his notice at Delta Air Lines and headed back to the Appalachians. He'd been in the Rockies, the Alps, the Grand Tetons, even the Catskills, but nothing made him feel cozy and comfortable the way the Alleghany ridges did. These mountains—hills, technically, given that most of the topography was erosional rather than tectonic—were soft and soothing the way no other landscape was.

He'd left, but they'd kept the light on, waiting patiently for his return.

Tony rolled his window down, breathing in the crisp, clean air. Mostly clean. A whiff of coal smoke from the old log cabin he was passing filled his nose with sulfur and probably a dozen other poisonous gases. But that was all right too. Like the rolling landscape around him, coal fires meant home.

And the people here could use his skills. Most IT consultants stuck to the cities, and a whole lot of folks didn't know how to properly break their home computers down for a trip to the shop, let alone how to discuss their business computer requirements.

Tony had done well with his house in Atlanta, a charming old Craftsman bungalow he'd bought in the seedy part of town before gentrification hit. Between the profit on the sale and the nest egg he'd put by during his corporate years, he'd come back home and retired.

Sort of.

He figured it would happen. Not long after he moved into his grandparents' old homeplace, family and then family friends started hitting him up, asking him to fix their internet connections, their dead computers, give advice on new monitors, and all the rest.

So he'd figured out how to stay busy, how to help people out, and how to earn a little extra in the process. These days, he spent his time going to people's homes and businesses, troubleshooting and repairing on the spot if he could, or taking notes and coming back later with the necessary parts and equipment if he couldn't.

He might be the only IT professional that made house calls in this neck of the woods.

Today he was heading to Holly Creek, to install and configure the new VPN client required for access to a legal database. Shouldn't take more than a few minutes, unless the config got extra persnickety, and he could hit the hiking trail out by Estonoa Lake afterward.

He turned off the highway and into Holly Creek, driving under the train trestle and turning left at the post office. Right on time.

One big difference between the coalfields and Atlanta? Ten miles meant ten minutes, not an hour or more.

He spotted the building with no problem. A three story brick job, like most of the old downtown buildings, but this one had a huge grand opening banner for the museum he'd been hearing about. Might have to check it out before his hike.

Tony parked his Prius beside the office, and walked around to the front until he saw the

Holbrook Law Office sign. No grand wooden panel with carving and gilt, this sign had to be snuck up on. Barely bigger than the toy license plate on a kid's bicycle.

He liked it.

Tony went inside, smiling as a shiny brass bell hung on the door announced his presence. The secretary or receptionist or whatever must've been surprised, because the first thing she did was choke on her donut.

He did his best to wait patiently as the secretary tried to get her food down. He also did his best to not chuckle or even crack a grin. Poor lady was probably embarrassed as all hell, and no point making it worse.

Besides, she sure was cute. About his age, he reckoned. Maybe a whisker younger. That chestnut hair of hers was clean and brushed, but not primped. No makeup to hide her face, either. Even from here he could pick up the aroma of clean skin and shampoo, no hint of smelly perfume. And she dressed comfortable, not classy.

No ring, not that a ringless finger meant single.

Ah well. Not like he'd be asking her out anyway.

Tony kept fit, and had enough vain in him to reckon he looked okay. But he'd been the short kid in school until he hit his growth around sixteen.

That was also the first time his body had managed to stretch his youthful flab into something a little less round.

He'd also been the school egghead. Between his mom trotting him out at parties to impress her friends with math tricks and trivia, and having to hide from all the boys who thought he was too smart for his own good, he'd learned early to hide his intelligence. Even after years spent engineering networks and building servers, he still had trouble not playing the dumb hillbilly.

And he'd never figured out the trick of talking to women. Still too damn shy for his own good.

Oh, he'd had his share of dates. Even a couple of flings that lasted a month or two. The inevitable breakups were probably his own fault. He always ended up with women who didn't read, couldn't talk about anything other than their jobs, or their clothes, or whatever dipshit TV show was the latest trendy thing to watch. No one who could hold a real conversation about anything interesting to him.

He'd given up a while back, decided the bachelor life wasn't so bad.

The counter girl finally washed the rest of her bite down.

"You okay now, miss?"

"I'm…I'm fine, thank you," she said, only coughing a little. "What can I do for you today?"

"I reckon I'm here to do something for you, or your boss at least," he said. "I have an appointment with the lawyer, Ms. Holbrook, to get her online with the new version of LexisNexis. Is she here, or when you reckon she'll be back?"

CHAPTER 3

Okay, this guy's cuteness factor had just dropped. He assumed she was the receptionist? Just because she was sitting at the reception desk?

Yeah, yeah. But she could have a little fun.

"I think Ms. Holbrook was expecting the actual IT *professional*," she said, dousing her words in as much saccharin as she could. "You know, someone in a suit and tie? Perhaps with a designer pocket protector?"

She immediately regretted her snark as an amazing shade of red crept up his face.

"Please, I'm sorry," she said, standing and offering her hand. "I'm Amy Holbrook. You must be Anthony with 'Your Place or Ours.'"

He hesitated, the color fading a little. Then her hand disappeared in his as he shook with her.

"Yes ma'am," he said, releasing her hand. "But it's just Tony."

"Oh god. *Please* don't call me ma'am. I'm Amy. Come on back, I'll show you where the library is."

She took him to the research room and pointed out the Mac that was set up for LexisNexis. He gave the machine a quick glance, then turned and stared at the floor-to-ceiling bookcases lining the far wall. Copies of the Code of Virginia filled the shelves, their bindings more yellow than tan these days.

"Y'all still use these?" He pulled out one of the hoary old books, and sneezed when dust rose.

"Yes we do," she said, smiling. "But only for decoration. And because no one trusts a lawyer or a doctor who doesn't have a wall full of sleep medicine."

Tony laughed. An honest, open laugh that sent a tingle through her. She liked that laugh, yes she did. And they way it lit up his whole face, making his eyes—

Down girl, down. Bad lawyer!

"I've written down the passwords for the admin account and the LexisNexis portal," she said, hoping he couldn't see the sudden heat in her cheeks.

"I appreciate that, ma...Amy." He sat at the desk and cracked his knuckles. "Always best when I don't have to hack my way in and make you beg me for the new password."

"And what makes you think I wouldn't hack along right behind you?"

Tony smiled up at her.

"You know computer systems?"

"I should. I designed and built the original network here when I was in college. Lasted until my uncle retired and I finally got the chance to bring things into this century. I haven't kept up with tech stuff since I started doing law, so I called you to do the VPN, instead of breaking a depreciable asset."

He gave her a look, one she decided was good, then ran his hands up the wall above the network jack.

"Who pulled the cabling?"

"I did," she said. She still got a thrill of pride at the smooth walls. Her uncle's best friend was a carpenter, and he said he had to use a magnifying glass to find the channels she'd cut and then patched.

"Good work," he said. "Damn good work. These old building can be a bear when you get up in the ceiling or inside the walls."

CHAPTER 4

Tony wasn't kidding about the work. Replastering these old lathboard walls wasn't for the faint of heart. Not to mention getting up in the ceilings with who knew how many decades of rats, mice, squirrels, and who knew what had lived their lives. There were enough framed paintings and photos on the walls that most mistakes wouldn't be visible, but he had the idea that if he pulled them all down, he still wouldn't find many blemishes.

He looked up and saw her smiling as she ran her own hand over the wall.

He'd thought she was cute when he first saw her. With that memory smile on her face, the pride she still obviously had in her college-age work, she was downright beautiful.

Something had been tickling at the back of his

brain ever since he'd gotten this job. It finally clicked when she saw a photograph on the wall of a young man in slacks and a golf shirt addressing a panel of starchy old coots.

"Holbrook," he said. "Is your uncle Jay Holbrook, by chance?"

"Yes he is. Do you know him? I think everybody must."

"We never met, but I wrote him a letter way back, when I first read about the Reclamation Warriors and how he went to DC and made 'em pass some decent laws. I remember that picture from the article. He sent me a lovely reply, wrote to me like I was an equal and not just a little kid."

"That was in 1977," she said, one eyebrow rising. "Just how old *are* you, Mr. Anthony Holbrook?"

"Aw, I was in third grade, so I reckon I read about him in '92 or so."

"A third grader interested in conservation history and law? My, my, my." She smiled again, but it wasn't the smile of memory. She was looking right at him.

Tony yanked his eyes back to the machine, hoping his hands weren't shaking as brought the Finder up and began the laborious task of navigating the LexisNexis virtual private network configuration.

CHAPTER 5

Amy left Tony to his work, but couldn't help herself peeking in from time to time. She didn't want to disturb him, but she needn't have worried.

He sat there muttering now and then as he whisked through the various pages and dialog boxes, staring fixedly at the screen with all the open-eyed focus of Bella when the chicken came out.

She was thinking about those shoulders when he came out of the library with that satisfied look that only computer geeks after a successful foray seem to have.

"All set, Amy. I put the icon right in the middle of the screen, can't miss it."

"Thank you, Tony. Do you invoice, or shall I pay you now?"

Tony pulled out a pocket watch, glanced at it, then put it back in his jeans.

"Well, it only took about twenty minutes. At my usual rate, that works out to about forty bucks. I don't think that'll make a difference in my dinner plans, so an invoice is just fine."

Again with that damn *smile* of his.

"I don't think it'll break our bank either. I'm afraid the only cash I have is a fifty, and we're out of checks until tomorrow."

"I ain't got any change," he said, scratching his beard. "Tell you what. How about I run across the street to the Western Front, grab a chunk of 'mater pie for my lunch? I won't be just a minute, and we can settle up then."

"I'll go with you," she said, wondering where *that* idea came from. "My donut didn't last long, and I could stand to stretch my legs."

He seemed to hesitate, his eyes flicking everywhere but on her, and she mentally kicked herself. But then he relaxed.

"Sure, that'd be great."

He held the front door for her, and followed her into the street.

"Say, I hope you don't think I'm too nosy, but I saw your bachelor's diploma in yonder. Didn't see your law school one. Where'd you do your legal?"

"I didn't go to law school. I studied under my uncle while I worked here during college. I thought

I was going to be an English Lit professor, but I fell in love with this instead."

She waited to see what his reaction would be. Some people thought not going to law school meant she hadn't been able to get in.

He was walking beside her, looking around at the new construction and the old buildings. His hands were in his pockets, and he seemed perfectly at ease.

"Sounds like me," he finally said. "I was a Lit boy, myself. Actually, double majors in Lit and ancient history, with double minors in PoliSci and German. Didn't finish any of it, though."

"Why not?" she asked, as they turned the corner. The aromas coming from the hotel's restaurant had her tummy grumbling. She wanted to keep him talking to cover up the noise.

"Well, all those programs are great if a body wants to teach. I couldn't see me grading a bunch of papers, and I really didn't want to spend my life asking if you want fries with that, so I took some time off. Went down to Atlanta to work a while. Earn some money while I decided what to be when I grew up."

"And now you do computer work?"

"Yep. I was working for a little publishing company, doing data entry. I've been messing with computers since right about the time I sent Mr. Holbrook that letter I told you about. Saw an invoice for a new system, told the boss how she could save a few hundred bucks shaving off options they didn't need. She made me the office IT guy on the spot. After that I started studying, taking contract work here and there as I learned more."

"So you're self-taught too, huh?"

"Yeah. I got my certifications, worked my way up through the ranks until the only next step was management. I had no interest in that, so I came back here. It's a good gig. I get to play with computers without being locked into one tiny niche. And I get to put a smile on people's faces."

They went in, had great food and even better conversation. They talked about their favorite books and movies, realized their iTunes libraries had an awful lot in common. Tony had her and the rest of the diners in stitches when he stood up, pulled his pants up nearly to his sternum, shoved his hips forward and slumped his shoulders to do his "Billy Bob Shakespeare." Amy could just see the biballs and straw hat.

"Ta be, er not ta be. That there's the question. Whether hit's better in yo' haid to suffer the slangs and arrers of piss-poor luck, or to whup up on them sumbitches and give 'em what fer! To croak, to pass plumb out..."

Wow. He knew Hamlet's entire soliloquy.

Everyone applauded as Tony bowed and took

his seat. Wiping the tears away, Amy couldn't help thinking she might be in trouble with this one.

"What time you got to be back at the office?" he asked, his hand sliding forward on the table, then jerking back.

Now what did that mean, exactly?

"I'm the boss. I'll be there when I get there."

CHAPTER 6

Tony was having trouble keeping his brains between his ears. He couldn't believe he'd done the Shakespeare thing in front of a crowd of strangers.

But it made Amy laugh. And he *liked* her laugh. A lot.

And her smile.

He chewed the inside of his cheeks as the waiter brought his change.

"Say, uh, Amy. I was wondering…well…"

"Yes?"

"I saw that the Lyric is showing a Monty Python double feature matinee. *And Now for Something Completely Different* and *Life of Brian*. I don't have any more calls today. I wonder if I might could treat you to some popcorn and a Coke?"

He tried to discreetly wipe his palms on his jeans.

Amy's face lit up with that smile again.

"Oh, I *love* Python! You're on, big boy. But be warned. I can out-quote you with my eyes closed."

His heart skipped a beat, then settled back down. His own face busted open in a grin so big she could probably count his fillings.

"You think so, do you? Well, we'll just see about that, missy!"

CHAPTER 7

*A*my hadn't laughed so much in one day in…well, in never, truth be told. For all his country accent and "aw, shucks" manner, Tony was the most intelligent man she'd met in a long, long time. At least who wasn't family.

As he'd relaxed, his smile came out more and more. They'd spent the afternoon trying to one-up each other, saying the next line before the characters on screen could.

It was a close thing, but she was sure she'd won.

After the movies, they returned to the office so she could change into a pair of boots, then went out on the trail before the sun went down. He told her about every plant and tree they passed, and she got to educate him on which birds were singing.

Their shoulders brushed occasionally, and if that

was an accident on his part, it certainly wasn't on hers.

By the time they finished their walk, she was sure.

She was *definitely* in trouble with this one.

CHAPTER 8

is hand itched to take hers. But dammit, they'd just met!

But he could talk to her. Without stammering or needing to crack stupid jokes left and right.

Okay, he'd cracked a couple. Which made her either laugh or roll her eyes. Or both.

They walked for nearly three miles, but he felt like the day had flown by. The moon was just peeking over the ridge when they finally made it back to the office parking lot, and his car.

What the hell did he do now? He'd never had much practice at this.

She leaned against the wall and he stood by the car. The ease between them was gone for some reason.

Tony put his hands in his pockets. Pulled them back out.

Amy just leaned against the wall, staring at him, chewing her lower lip.

"You okay?" he finally managed. "Why are you biting your lip?"

"I guess that's something you'll have to figure out."

She smiled at him again, and this smile didn't light her face up.

This smile set him on fire. Was she…

Slowly Tony took a step toward Amy. She reached out and put her hands on his hips.

Somehow his own hands were on her shoulders.

She was still leaning on the wall, and he couldn't help but lean in with her, until their eyes and lips were only millimeters apart.

OVER THE DECADES TO COME, Amy and Tony would often debate who kissed who that night.

But Amy knew. Yes she did. *She* had kissed *him*.

Tony wasn't sure about that, but he was damn sure of one thing.

He'd never looked back.

Thank you for joining us for these first steps on the path to Happily Ever After! We hope you enjoyed reading as much as we enjoyed writing them.

For more from Jason A. Adams and Kari Kilgore, turn the page or visit www.SpiralPublishing.net/Romance.

ALSO BY KARI KILGORE

I hope you enjoyed reading the stories collected here in *Partners in Romance* as much as we enjoyed writing them. If you're in the mood for more romance, swing by www.KariKilgore.com/Romance.

For more tales with LGBTQ+ characters in almost every genre, head over to www.KariKilgore.com/LGBTQStories.

For more stories where speculative elements are either slight or not there at all, head over to www.KariKilgore.com/ContemporaryFiction.

Check out more of my fiction, including almost every genre, and be first to hear about release dates, Kickstarters and other fun projects, and exclusive e-book and print editions at www.KariKilgore.com.

Romance:

Protecting Her Own

The Coffee Bomb and the Corporate Spy

The Box of Possibilities

Escape into Romance

Stories with Strong Romantic Elements:

The Voices through Time Series:

Songs in the Mountain

Secrets in the Land

Sorrows in the Earth

Walking the Ghosts

The Odd Society:

Independent by Means of Magic

Protected by Means of Magic

The Storms of Future Past Series:

Dreaming the Storm

Joining the Storm

Into the Storm

Fighting the Storm

Storms of the Heart

Storms of Future Past Omnibus

Collections:

Investigations Beyond Belief

A Tapestry of Holiday Tales

Novels:

Until Death

The Dream Thief

Hand Me Downs

The Great Gold Record Heist

Novellas:

Legacy of the Land

In the Pines

Fantastic Women: A Dark Fantasy Novella Trio

DNA Never Lies

Murder at the Fabulous Feline Emporium

Team Building Revenge

Dispatches from the Galaxy:

Restricted Species

The Becalmed

Plurapod Pathogen

The Changes Cascade

Near Future Forward (with Jason A. Adams)

Dispatches from the Galaxy: A Space Opera Novella Trio

Dangerous Days on a Pleasure Planet

Collections:

Fantastic Shorts: Volume 1

Fantastic Shorts: Volume 2

Fantastic Shorts: Volume 3

Stepping Out of Reality

Facing Down Extraordinary

Hacking Cybercrime

Passages in the Real World

Fantastic Side Trips

A Kaleidoscope of Cat Tales

Aunties Among Us

Four-Legged Heroes

Anthologies with Jason A. Adams:

Shadows Mountain Deep

Uncommon Holidays

Partnership in Crime

ALSO BY JASON A. ADAMS

I hope you enjoyed reading the stories in *Partners in Romance* as much as we enjoyed writing them.

Visit www.JasonAdamsBooks.com and join the adventure for exclusive new fiction, my past and future travels, and whatever else strikes my fancy. Hope to see you there!

Novellas:

Agonist

Collections and Anthologies:

Normally Fantastic

On the Case!

Capeless Heroes

Through the Squirrel Tree

Tales From the Squirrel Garden: Volume 1

(with Kari Kilgore)

Partnership in Crime

Shadows Mountain Deep

Near Future Forward

Uncommon Holidays

ABOUT KARI

Kari and her husband Jason A. Adams met in a computer lab in college in 1990 and proceeded to live out several enduring romance tropes, including rebound romance, friends into lovers, young love, and even second chance romance when they divorced and remarried, all before the end of the 90s. So it was perhaps inevitable that they'd both end up writing romance.

While none of the stories in *Partners in Romance* are completely autobiographical, there are hints of truth in all of them.

Kari writes romance, contemporary fiction, fantasy, mystery, and science fiction, and she's happiest when she surprises herself. She lives with Jason, various house critters, and wildlife they're better off not knowing more about.

The Confidential Adventure Club

For Kari's exclusive free After The End stories and deleted scenes, discounts, early releases, adorable pet photos, Kickstarters and other fun projects, Spiral Publishing Exclusive Edition ebooks and print books, and a whole lot more not available anywhere else, join us in The Club.

Hope to see you there!

www.KariKilgore.com
www.SpiralPublishing.net
www.ConfidentialAdventureClub.com

BB bookbub.com/authors/kari-kilgore

a amazon.com/author/karikilgore

g goodreads.com/karikilgore

f facebook.com/kari.kilgore.1

ABOUT JASON

Jason A. Adams writes across the spectrum. His stories include science fiction, fantasy, horror, Appalachian folk tales, and romance, of course.

You can find more of his work at www.JasonAdamsBooks.com.

Jason's stories also appear in several issues of *Pulphouse Magazine, Mystery, Crime, and Mayhem, Uncollected Anthology, Thrill Ride,* and WMG Publishing's Holiday Spectaculars.

Jason, a recovering Air Force brat who grew up all over the US and Japan, now perches in the mountains of Southwest Virginia with his excellent author wife Kari Kilgore (www.KariKilgore.com), several spoiled-rotten house critters, and assorted wild visitors from the nearby forest.

news@JasonAdamsBooks.com

 facebook.com/Jason.A.Adams.2

ADDITIONAL COPYRIGHT INFORMATION